The Mystery of Babylon

WILLIAM DIXON

The Mystery of Babylon

Inquiries should be addressed to

FRONTERA PUBLISHING COMPANY
P. O. Box 80112
Austin, Texas 78708
www.mysterybabylon.org

FIRST EDITION: 2009

ISBN: 978-0-615-29411-7

Cover design by Rebecca Byrd Bretz

All Bible quotes are from the New International Version

Printed in the United States of America
at Morgan Printing in Austin, Texas

TABLE OF CONTENTS

PROLOGUE

"One of the seven angels who had the seven bowls came and said to me, 'Come, I will show you the punishment of the great prostitute, who sits on many waters. With her the kings of the earth committed adultery and the inhabitants of the earth were intoxicated with the wine of her adulteries.'

Then the angel carried me away in the spirit into a desert. There I saw a woman sitting on a scarlet beast that was covered with blasphemous names and had seven heads and ten horns. The woman was dressed in purple and scarlet, and was glittering with gold, precious stones and pearls. She held a golden cup in her hand, filled with abominable things and the filth of her adulteries. This title was written on her forehead:

MYSTERY — BABYLON THE GREAT
THE MOTHER OF PROSTITUTES
AND OF THE ABOMINATIONS OF THE EARTH.

I saw that the woman was drunk with the blood of the saints, the blood of those who bore testimony to Jesus."

REVELATION 17:1-6

These amazing verses from the Bible have been interpreted for many centuries as either referring to the Roman Catholic Church or a global apostate religious system that will come into being during the period of human history the Bible calls the "end times" or "latter days". In support of these views are

v

Scripture passages such as Revelation 17:9 which say that the woman referred to in the verses above resides in a city built on seven hills — universally recognized as Rome; and Revelation Chapter 13, which describes a religious system to be established by the leaders known as the Antichrist and the False Prophet.

We know, however, that any global system, whether governmental, economic, or religious, must have a beginning or foundation upon which developmental stages follow. In other words, a global system does not simply spring into existence fully developed. The implication of this is that, whatever "Mystery Babylon" is, it had a beginning, followed by developmental stages, and it will someday come into full fruition. Revelation 17:1-6 describes a system that has come into full fruition, with a global reach, and is ready for God's judgment.

What, then, has provided the foundation for Mystery Babylon? Was it the obvious mixture of paganism with Christianity at Rome? Of the multitude of examples that support this, consider just two. The Pope is called "Pontifex Maximus", which means "The Supreme Bridge-Keeper". Why such an unusual title? The answer is shocking. Pontifex Maximus was the title of the high priest of the cult of Janus in Rome before the arrival of Christianity! Around 60 B.C. the Roman emperors began adopting this title as an expression of their supposed divine authority as Emperor and High Priest of the sacred mysteries. The one thus endowed with the title Pontifex Maximus, whether high priest, emperor, or both combined, declared himself to be the one who stood as the bridge, or mediator, between mankind and the gods, with the power of determining the ultimate destiny of souls. When Christianity became established in Rome, the Bishop of Rome — the Pope —

simply adopted the title and many of the functions of the pagan high priests and emperors.

Where does the worship of Mary originate? It is not found in the Bible. Jesus never said to worship, or adore, his mother. In fact, in Matthew 4:10 Jesus says "Worship the Lord your God, and serve him only." If Mary worship is not authorized by the Bible, then where did it come from? Again, the answer is shocking. The pagan religions of the Middle East and Mediterranean areas all included the worship of female deities. The chief female deity was always worshipped, and adored, as the "Queen of Heaven". In an effort to win converts, the early Church fathers took that title and applied it to Mary, the mother of Jesus.

What else could have provided the foundation for Mystery Babylon? In our own times the quintessential global organization is, of course, the United Nations. Most people do not realize that, since the year 2000, the United Nations has promoted and sponsored an organization called the United Religions Initiative, which strives to bring all of the world's religions together as one. Why is this not generally known? Because the media does not cover it. Why does the media not cover it? The powers that be don't want it known… yet. It is a beast waiting to be unleashed. Anyone who utters criticism of this monstrosity will be called intolerant, divisive, bigoted, and self-righteous.

Worldwide computer systems now, for the first time in history, make it possible for every human to be identified and cataloged. We also seem to be rapidly moving toward becoming a cashless society, where all one needs to purchase something is a number. Optical scanning technology, combined with computer systems, are making cash and checks obsolete. Now we are seeing the microchipping of human beings with computer chips inserted under the skin. These microchips can, and will, contain our personal information — medical, legal, and financial. Once a person is microchipped they can be tracked and found anywhere in the world they go.

Is it not chilling to realize that the New Testament Book of Revelation predicts, in chapter 13, that a future world leader will require that every person be given a mark, or number, and that without it no one can buy or sell anything? The human author of the Book of Revelation lived over 1,900 years ago. Is it even conceivable that he could have foreseen the advent of technology that would make his prediction a reality? Why would such an outlandish notion even occur to him? What are the mathematical odds that his prediction would come true?

It is not "conspiracy theory nonsense" to acknowledge that global forces — political, economic, and religious — are extending their reach around the world and into our personal lives as never before in history. In fact, it may very well be myopic and naïve not to recognize it.

We are not being liberated. Our freedoms are dwindling.

The goal of a world government and a unified global religious system, supposedly in the name of equality and unity, has existed since ancient times. As strange and somber as it may sound, these concepts, along with the religious practices described above, had their origin in ancient Babylon. That great city was founded by a man named Ninus whose adopted title was Nimrod, which meant 'the rebel'. Together with his wife, Semiramis, Nimrod built the world's first empire along with its first man-made religion.

But something else happened in Babylon. For reasons not fully understood, the tribes and clans living in and around Babylon were compelled to leave. From there they migrated to all parts of the earth, and took their corrupted religious system with them.

This author has come to the conclusion that the mystery of Babylon is something far, far more pervasive than any existing religious organization or the United Nations. It includes those entities but is not confined to them. The true mystery of Babylon reaches from the concrete canyons of New York City, London, and Tokyo to the most isolated tribes and ethnic groups on the earth. It has under its influence tribal shamans in Siberia as well as priests in the cathedrals of Europe. It includes witch doctors, ministers, and imams among all the scattered peoples of the earth. In all instances its practitioners seek spiritual knowledge and enlightenment by means other than submission and obedience to the God of the Bible who declares emphatically that apart from him there are no gods.

The academic explanation for the world's religions is that they are an attempt by ignorant primitive people to explain things in nature that they can't understand. But who would invent a spirit being to represent, for example the sun, give the being a name and attributes, and then worship him, knowing that the whole concept is false? Such a system would eventually be exposed as baseless and contrived and would be discarded. And why does religion still thrive, even in the technologically advanced countries? Are we really still ignorant and primitive? It seems humans are religious creatures even though they *do* understand the forces of nature.

No, there is more to it. It is not a coincidence that a Queen of Heaven has been worshipped all over the world by tribes and ethnic groups who never had contact with one another. Nor is it a coincidence that the common elements of the world's religions are now being woven together in an attempt to create a one-world religion.

The forces behind the drive toward one-world government and one-world religion are bringing to fruition the mystery of Babylon.

Finally, consider what the Bible actually says concerning the spirit beings we know as Satan, or the devil, and his angels:

- Three times he is called the 'prince of this world' by Jesus Christ. (John 12:31, 14:30, and 16:11)
- The whole world is under his control. (1 John 5:19)
- He is the 'god' of this age. (2 Corinthians 4:4)
- He is the 'ruler of the kingdom of the air'. (Ephesians 2:2)
- The kingdoms of the world are his. (Luke 4:5,6)
- He is the 'serpent' that deceives humans. (Genesis 3:1-5)
- He roams throughout the earth at will. (Job 1:7)
- He leads the whole world astray (!). (Revelation 12:9)
- He is the deceiver of the nations. (Revelation 20:3)

If these teachings from the Bible concerning our spiritual enemies are false, then put the Bible up on the shelf along with Grimm's Fairy Tales and be done with it. If, however, the teachings are true, then we should be alert and watchful. For the Bible also teaches that something dreadful happened in Babylon in ancient times, resulting in God scattering the people to all parts of the earth. It was spiritual rebellion they were guilty of. It resulted in a corrupt religious system, filled with occult beliefs, that has spread all over the world and has touched every human being.

Revelation 17:5 speaks of the mystery of Babylon the Great, referring to something begun long ago, but yet to reach its fulfillment and complete presentation to the waiting world. The words 'Mystery, Babylon the Great' were not chosen haphazardly. The words are to be taken very literally and very seriously.

Μυστεριον Βαβυλον ε Μεγαλε ε ματερ τον πορνον και τον βδελυγματον τεσ γεσ

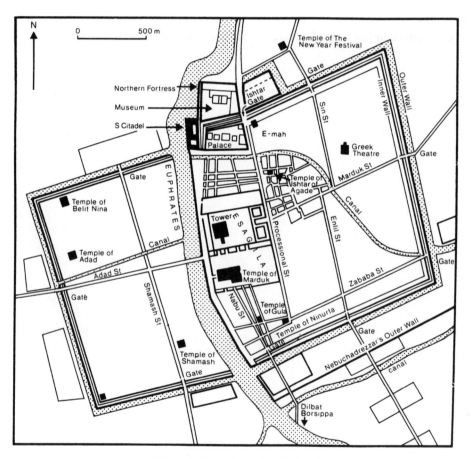

Map of the City of Babylon

Babylon was a gold cup

in the Lord's hand;

she made the whole earth drunk.

The nations drank her wine;

therefore they

have now gone mad.

JEREMIAH 51:7

CHAPTER ONE

Chulgomet and the Flood

The spirit Chulgomet stared from his vantage point on a towering cliff and spewed foul curses. As he watched in dismay, the churning floodwaters rose above the treetops. Torrential rainfall, never before seen by humans or angels, poured relentlessly from the dark, menacing heavens. The rising waters seemed to merge with the sky as lightning streaked in every direction, followed by crescendos of thunder. The wind howled deafeningly, stirring up enormous waterspouts, and it seemed to Chulgomet as though the Creator himself had grabbed hold of the Earth and had violently shaken the oceans out of their assigned places.

Throngs of human creatures floated on the surface, clinging desperately to debris, and each other, only to be swept under by the roiling torrents. Even those seeking refuge in the high places of the hills and mountains were swept away. Their sacred high places, where they chose to worship beings who were not gods, offered no refuge.

Chulgomet raged aloud:

"This is ours!
The Earth belongs to us!
We made it ours!
We are the gods of Earth and its inhabitants!"

As he ranted and blasphemed, he noted another presence appearing before him. It was Naath, a repulsive little messenger spirit, reporting to Chulgomet as ordered.

"Lord Chulgomet," he croaked, frog-like, "it is as you feared. The destruction you see before you spares no part of the planet. Our work is ruined! And the humans were worshipping us instead of God! They called us the Nephilim — the ones cast down from above."

"Cast down," Naath repeated to himself, slowly realizing that the term was derogatory. Shaking it off, he continued, while Chulgomet stared at him disgustedly. "We had some interesting times mingling with the humans, especially the females, right Lord Chulgomet? Why we even had them... ."

But he never finished the question, for Chulgomet raised his hand toward Naath, who was instantly knocked off the precipice and soared spinning head over heels, hundreds of yards away, finally disappearing into the gray churning waters.

"Disgusting rodent," Chulgomet chuckled, momentarily pleased with himself.

He soon returned to his brooding.

"The little monster was right" he mused. "We *had* twisted things pretty much to our design. Our master Lucifer *was* very pleased. Truly, the human creatures were designed by the Creator in his own spiritual image, but we diverted them from their original purpose of loving God and fellowshipping with him."

"How easy it was," he gloated, "to trick them into worshipping *us*; a few simple tricks, a 'ghostly' manifestation here and there, whispered suggestions, and... behold! We have taken the place of God!"

It had been an astonishingly simple matter for Lucifer, the chief of all the fallen spirits, to seduce and deceive the prototype humans, Adam and Eve, away from obedience to their Creator. God had placed them in Eden, a paradise on Earth. He made them stewards of his earthly creation and set only one restriction on them. He warned them "You must not eat from the tree of the knowledge of good and evil, for when you eat of it you will surely die!" indicating spiritual death and separation from God.

There was, in other words, knowledge that was forbidden for humans.

Lucifer's plan was thus devised. First, confuse them as to what it was, exactly, that God forbade them to do. This was accomplished by distorting the simple and direct commandment of God that was given to them. Next, make them desire the forbidden thing by appealing to them through their fleshly senses. Finally, poison their faith through the lie that God had withheld something from them that was actually good, something that would make them *like God himself!*

A great snare was now in place, one that the fallen spirits would use to lead humanity away from God. For of all the gifts and abilities the Creator had bestowed upon the original human parents, of the utmost importance, indeed of eternal importance, was that most astonishing endowment called free will. Free will meant that each person would possess, as each angelic being already did, the ability to choose whether to follow God's will or his or her own will. The Creator took a great risk in endowing his heavenly and earthly creations with this capability. For now not only angels but humans could exert their wills against the will of God.

Behind it all was this: he wanted to be loved and honored, not by robotic beings who had no choice in the matter, for that would not be real love. No, for love to be real, it had to be expressed through a free will choice. Therein lay the risk; would beings thus endowed choose for him or against him?

The momentous event that transpired in Eden was known in both Heaven and Earth simply as The Fall. All of creation knew the story. The Rebel Lucifer had only to dangle an enticement in front of the newly created humans, something that would appeal to the same instinct that led to the downfall of Lucifer himself... pride!

Not *thy* will God, but *mine!*

The plan worked.

Eve was deceived while Adam willfully disobeyed. They reached out and took hold of what was expressly forbidden and fell from God's grace. They were now subject to toil, pain, sickness and death. They were also expelled from Eden. Thereafter it did not take long for the descendents of Adam and Eve to turn away from their heavenly Father and begin worshipping and exalting the creation rather than the Creator himself.

They soon personified every aspect of nature as deities. The wind, rain, sky, sun, moon, fertility, life, death, even the earth itself, were adored and placated for health, sustenance and blessing. They knew God, but did not glorify him or give thanks to him. Their thinking thus became corrupted and their hearts darkened. They became fools, and exchanged the glory of God for images of men and animals, things made of wood, stone, gold, and silver; things that could not talk, walk, or breathe. But behind these idols there lurked an invisible and intelligent, yet malignant, being who was dedicated to opposing God and wrecking humans. Beings created in the spiritual image of God, made for fellowship with him, became utterly corrupted and beyond restoration.

A searing jolt of condemnation and judgment wracked Chulgomet as he pondered these things. After all, he and other myriads of angelic beings had once occupied exalted positions in the heavenly realms. Then a movement had surged among some of the angels, led by the foremost of God's creation — the wondrous and beautiful Lucifer — who ministered at the very throne of God as Covering Cherub.

Chulgomet now began to tremble with pride as he recalled Lucifer bellowing in a terrifying outburst that tore asunder both time and space:

> "*I WILL ascend to heaven,*
> *I WILL exalt my throne above the stars of God;*
> *I WILL sit enthroned on the mount of assembly, on the utmost heights of the North.*
> *I WILL ascend above the tops of the clouds;*
> *I WILL make myself like the Most High God!*"

Chulgomet would never forget what happened next. For there was no sound or movement in the universe following Lucifer's rebellious tirade. All life and motion froze in suspense as the sentient creation awaited a response from God Almighty.

The wait wasn't long.

Lucifer, and every other spirit who sided with him, were instantly ejected from the heavenly realms, and like falling stars they tumbled in complete disgrace to Earth, to which they were now confined as in a prison.

Then was heard by all creation, not the terrible voice of

vengeance that all expected, nor the sudden annihilation of Lucifer and his fellow rebels.

All of the heavenly creation sensed the voice of One, not caught off-guard and outraged by the revelation of unprovoked rebellion, but rather the saddened voice of One who knew, from endless eons past, that his love and trust were to be betrayed by one upon whom very great and unprecedented honor had been bestowed. The still, powerful voice addressed Lucifer, the leader of the rebellion, for all to hear:

> "You were the model of perfection, full of wisdom and
> perfect in beauty. You were in Eden, the Garden of God;
> every precious stone adorned you. You were anointed
> as a guardian cherub, for so I ordained you. You were
> on the holy mount of God; you walked among the fiery
> stones. You were blameless in your ways from the
> day you were created till wickedness was found in you.
>
> Through your widespread trade you were filled with
> violence, and you sinned. So I drove you in disgrace
> from the mount of God, and I expelled you, O guardian
> cherub, from among the fiery stones. Your heart became
> proud on account of your beauty, and you corrupted your
> wisdom because of your splendor. So I threw you to the
> earth; I made a spectacle of you before rulers."

At the memory of this, Chulgomet, seized now by an unseen and irresistible force, was thrown facedown to the ground. He groaned, knowing that his own willful sin in following Lucifer had left him condemned and without hope. Dazed but sternly unrepentant, he raised himself and scanned the area, hoping none of his underlings had seen him humiliated so.

No such luck. For his multi-dimensional sight caught glimpse of that fawning rat Naath, now joined by Moronth, a quarrelsome and untrustworthy fiend, flitting from the scene together, leering in Chulgomet's direction.

His thoughts of tormenting Naath and Moronth were suddenly interrupted by a shattering crack as the precipice Chulgomet stood upon gave way and crashed into the swirling, heaving ocean that now covered the planet. He hovered in the air where only moments before there had been a great majestic mountain.

Another spirit appeared. It was Asmera, one of his most brutal officials. Chulgomet looked him over, recalling that Asmera had once been an exceedingly beautiful being, wise and experienced beyond measure. Although he retained some of his original appearance, he was now — how would one say it — corrupted. His features were now terrible, not beautiful.

His wisdom was now directed toward mischief and violence rather than glorifying God and fulfilling the high commission he once had.

Asmera had become exceedingly adept at spiritual deception, and he exulted in his work, for he loathed and detested humans. He kept a careful account of the exact number of souls that he succeeded in seducing away from the Almighty One. He knew that once separated from God, a human could be chased down like a wounded or sick animal, separated from its herd, and could then be deceived and misled into every kind of abominable belief and practice. But at work in every instance was free will. The humans *chose* to disobey and reject their Creator. They *chose* to violate their God-given consciences and to dishonor themselves and their God.

Being beyond restoration, God, heartbroken, brought the forces of nature down on his creation to destroy it.

But a righteous remnant was found; a precious few who remained loyal to God.

Asmera gave his report:

"All is not lost, Lord Chulgomet. Not all of the humans have perished. There are survivors — eight of them to be precise — a man named Noah and his wife, and their sons and wives."

Hearing this, a smile made its way across Chulgomet's face.

"The battle continues!" he said. "We shall yet have humans to worship us!"

CHAPTER TWO

The Pristine Religion

Noah walked through the ark for what he assumed would be the last time. A feeling of wonderment mixed with nostalgia came over him as he breathed in the complex aromas he and his family had grown accustomed to since the flood began. The intense smell of many diverse animals, mingled with that of wood, tar and pitch made his head reel. He stood still and recalled that momentous day years ago when God spoke to him.

He was tending goats in the clover field by the curve in the stream. The Voice startled him and he whirled around to see who was speaking to him, although it was a Voice that was not so much heard as felt.

No one there!

Then the Voice began again,

"Noah! I am the God of your ancestors, and your God. With you I am pleased, for you seek to do that which is pleasing in my sight, obeying my laws written in the consciences of all who bear my image.

However, I have seen how great man's wickedness has become

on the Earth, that every inclination of his heart and mind are only evil all the time. Man is beyond healing. I am sorely grieved over my human creation and my own heart is filled with pain!

I have determined to destroy mankind which I have created from the face of the earth — all living creatures, both man and animal — for I am grieved that I have made them! But you Noah have found favor in my eyes.

You are to build a great boat, an ark, in the dimensions I will give to you. Make many rooms and stalls in it and coat it with pitch, inside and out. I am going to bring floodwaters upon the Earth to destroy all life, everything with the breath of life in it!

But I will establish my covenant with you. You, your wife, your sons and their wives, are to enter the ark. I will then bring to you a male and female of every species of animal that is to survive the coming catastrophe. You are to store away every kind of food you will need for yourselves and the animals."

Noah, lying with his face to the ground trembling, cried out "A flood? A boat? Destroy mankind? *What?*

What struggles he had to endure as he went about building the vessel God instructed him to build! His construction project became known far and wide and was universally ridiculed and scorned. Noah was an international laughingstock. His sons helped their father reluctantly. They were often nowhere to be found and Noah then worked alone. His poor wife tried to be supportive, but eventually began to treat her husband as though he had lost his mind. There were times Noah even wondered about himself.

Questioning thoughts ran through his mind. "Did I imagine the Voice? Was I ill that day? What is a 'flood'? Oh, if only the Voice of God would return to encourage me!"

But it never did.

Then the fateful day came that the sky fell and the seas overflowed their boundaries.

Noah's thoughts returned to the present as he reached out to pat the head of a friendly chattering monkey. He preferred not to think of the faces of those he had known for many years, panic-stricken as raging waters swept them and their families and homes away. However, he found himself in sad agreement with the judgment of his God concerning them. Their wickedness and idolatries were a continual pain to Noah and his family as they sought to remain faithful to God.

In all his dealings and his travels Noah knew *not one soul* who was not given over to worshipping things that were not God, as well as to the degrading of their bodies through perverse sexual practices.

Worst of all was the widespread practice of sacrificing their own children to demon 'gods' like Molech and Dagon.

Noah strained to bring to mind even one person, outside of his immediate family, who was loyal to God.

"Not even one," he shuddered. "The Lord is justified in his judgments."

Now the floodwaters had receded and the ground outside was drying out. It was time to leave the ark.

The women watched anxiously as Noah's sons, Shem and Japheth, lifted the post that secured the door to the main entrance of the ark.

What happened next was unforgettable.

As if hearing a command that the humans could not perceive, all of the animals began to pair up with their mates, even the crawling insects, and stood patiently as if awaiting further orders. Then they began to march parade-like down the massive gangplank. Upon touching the ground they continued on determinedly, without pausing or looking back, and fanned out in every direction until, hours later, they were all out of sight.

Now the time had come for Noah to do what God had laid on his heart.

His sons and their wives had already set up camp on dry ground when Noah summoned them to a small clearing in the trees nearby. He had erected an altar of uncut stone as God had instructed him, and as the rest of the little band of survivors bowed down with their faces to the ground, he offered a burnt sacrifice on it, thanking God for their deliverance. He then turned somberly to the small group, and indicating that they be seated on the ground, began to instruct them.

"My dear ones," he began slowly, "can there be any doubt that the mighty hand of the Holy One — El Shaddai — has been with us to preserve us alive from such a great destruction? You must understand why these things are, and what we are to do. For a heavy burden and responsibility has been laid upon us."

Noah continued. "The great God, the Creator of all that is, revealed to me the reason for the terrible judgment you have seen sweep over the earth!"

Noah now seemed to become larger than life, frightening his family with his fierce, riveting countenance.

"Listen to me!" He suddenly cried out, startling everyone. Listen I say!"

"Do not forget what I am about to tell you, or God himself will hold you accountable, and you have just witnessed his great and terrible power to judge and destroy!"

"Hear me now! There is one God — El Shaddai — the great, awesome and Holy One who has made everything that is! There are no other gods! It is because the people turned from him as disobedient children and were deceived and believed lies and worshipped things that were not God that this terrible destruction has come upon all the earth! They defiled their own bodies with their corrupt and unnatural practices."

"Never forget that it is he, in his infinite wisdom and power, who has made us. We did not make ourselves, nor did we spring from the soil or the oceans as an accident. But of the dust of the ground did he fashion Father Adam and placed him in a wondrous garden as the steward of God's earthly creation."

"All of the animals had their mates, except the man God had made. Seeing that it was not good for Father Adam to be alone, our gracious and loving Heavenly Father fashioned a woman from Adam's own body, a companion for him, and called her Eve, our Mother Eve. He presented her to Adam who declared 'This is now bone of my bone and flesh of my flesh; she shall be called Isha, woman, for she was taken out of Ish, man'.

"A great covenant was thus instituted for all humanity to come," Noah continued. "For God declared that a man shall leave his father and mother and be united to his wife, and that they would become *one flesh*. This is a great mystery for it speaks of God's spiritual union with those who are his own. For El Shaddai designed his human creation for a love relationship with himself. Yes, he greatly desires a voluntary love relationship with us. He himself has put this yearning within each man and woman. We resist this yearning and seek our own way at our peril, for just as God is spirit, so man's essential essence is also spirit. Spirit relates to spirit, and spirit rebels against spirit. He requires our obedience as children for our eternal good, that we may abide in his holy presence and love him forever."

"When a man dies, it is only the outer body that perishes; his spirit lives on — either *with* our heavenly Father, as reward, or *separated* from him, as punishment. Mark this well, never forget, it is our sins that separate us from God! It is not his will that anyone should be lost. His laws and precepts are engraved upon our consciences. When we willingly sin against him, seeking our own will rather than his perfect will, we are separated from him. Sin must be atoned for before sinful man can be reconciled with holy God!"

Noah lifted his head skyward, closed his eyes, and heaved a great sigh, as if overwhelmed with God's revelation. Then, returning his gaze to his little awestruck audience, he continued.

"My children, Father Adam and Mother Eve were created innocent. They wore no clothing and knew no shame. They existed for fellowship with our great God. They were placed in perfect surroundings, lacking nothing. But the Almighty One placed one restriction on them. He forbade them from taking of the fruit of the tree of the knowledge of good and evil, knowing that if they took of that fruit they would die spiritually."

"We know how they were willfully disobedient and were deceived by the evil one, the enemy of our souls. They thus rebelled against God, who had fashioned their essential essence according to his own spiritual image and had given them every good thing."

Noah now looked deeply pained. He continued.

"They were cast out of Eden, out of God's direct care, and sickness, pain, and death have been the lot of mankind ever since. We are also partakers of Father Adam and Mother Eve's nature," he said mournfully.

He hung his head and appeared to be choking back sobs of grief.

"For the inclination of man is to seek his own way rather than our loving Heavenly Father's way. Man cannot cure himself of this affliction!" Noah paused, steadying himself. His voice now rose, suddenly energized.

"Man is in need of a Redeemer, a Savior, to restore to him what has been lost!"

He then lowered his eyes and said, half to himself, "But, how a pure and holy God can forgive sin without compromising his own righteous character has not been revealed to me."

Shaking his head, he said, "This, however, *has* been shown me, that *apart from the shedding of blood there shall be no forgiveness of sins!* As for you, you shall approach your God through the sacrifice for the atonement of your sins, as I have just done in your sight. And you, my sons, must be the ministers of God for your families, in your homes. You shall make the sacrifice for the sins of your households, to make atonement between yourselves and our great God. You shall intercede on behalf of your families. As parents, you — husbands and wives — shall teach your children all these things so that they will not forget their God in heaven who loves them as a father loves his children.

"Now," he continued, "our great and mighty God has given us some final words of instruction before we leave this mountain. First of all, he has given us his promise that never again will he destroy all life with a flood, and he has set the multi-colored rainbow in the sky as a perpetual reminder of this promise. He has also instructed us and our descendants to be fruitful in childbearing and to fill the Earth. The fear of man shall be upon all the beasts of the Earth.

They are under our dominion. As God had previously given people the plants of the fields and the fruit of the trees, so now shall the animals also be our food.

"As for your fellowman, you shall not arbitrarily shed his blood. For whoever sheds the blood of man, by man shall his blood be shed; for in the image of God has God made man.

"My children, you and your descendants have been given a great responsibility and honor. You shall be stewards and caretakers of God's earthly creation!"

"Stewards and caretakers of God's earthly creation," the spirit Chulgomet mimicked sneeringly, only inches from Noah's face.

It was indeed a blessing that Noah and his loved ones could not see beyond the third dimension, for flocking all around them, above, below, and on all sides, were thousands of vicious spirits, of great authority and power, sent by Lucifer himself to review the state of things with the survivors of the flood.

Chulgomet turned and bellowed, beyond the hearing of the humans, "You have your orders! By any means necessary pervert the simple beliefs that God, our enemy, has placed in the hearts of the humans!

"You have heard Noah speak of man's desperate need for a Redeemer and Savior. So it is the eternal decree of God, whom we have despised, to provide such a Redeemer/Savior. The Creator is too kind to these loathsome creatures! They are only good for robbing, killing, and destroying! But *He* wants to give them *life*!

"Colleagues" he continued, "it is not enough to kill their bodies; we must lead them into spiritual rebellion against their Maker. They must not worship God. They must worship *us!* They will worship the sun and the moon, the stars, animals, each other, better yet, their *own selves...*anything but God!"

So Noah and his little band of survivors trekked down from the mountaintop their ark had come to rest upon. The land was open before them for there were no other humans to contend with. They eventually settled down and became hunters, herdsmen, and farmers.

Centuries passed, and the offspring of Noah's sons — Shem, Ham, and Japheth — increased greatly. The families became clans and the clans became tribes. As the land became overburdened with people, the tribes of the descendants of Noah drifted down from the mountains and hills onto the plain of Shinar, to be known in later times as Iraq, seeking better lands for their families, their livestock, and their crops.

There a man became great, a mighty hunter of men, the first to exert his will over his fellowman and to wage war against others to dominate them. His name was Ninus, but the people called him Nimrod, which meant 'rebel'.

He founded a city called Babylon.

CHAPTER THREE

The Watchers

Before the Great Flood there had been a thriving and
advanced civilization known as Sumer. This civilization
flourished to the south of the plain of Shinar where the great
Euphrates and Tigris rivers merge and empty into the Persian
Gulf. The Sumerians built great monumental cities — Eridu, Ur,
Ereck, Lakash, Borsippa, Nippur, Shurupak, Larsa, and others —
and were known to have possessed advanced knowledge in the arts
and sciences. The legends said that these people appeared quite
suddenly with their civilization and technology fully developed.
No traces of earlier developments were to be found.

How did the Sumerians obtain their advanced civilization,
which had no prior history?

An ominous answer lay hidden in the name of the land itself.
For Sumer, or Shumer, as the inhabitants pronounced it, meant
'Land of the Watchers'.

According to the legends these Watchers were heavenly beings
who came down from the skies and interacted with the people. For
this reason they were known as Nephilim, which meant 'those who
came down', or 'were cast down' to Earth. These beings, the stories
related, shared knowledge with the people concerning such things
as arts and sciences, and even taught them writing. But they also
demanded that the people worship them as gods, which indeed,
they seemed to be.

The Nephilim taught the people to worship a supreme being called Anu, the Father of the Gods, as well as many other gods, who were in fact not gods at all, but fallen angels, renegade spirits, yet intelligent and powerful. These were red-handed rebels, cast down from heaven to earth, hence their name, Nephilim. Finally, in defiance of their Creator, they set about wrecking his creation and leading humanity astray spiritually.

These beings presented themselves to the people of Sumer, and to later peoples, under many names and titles:

Enlil, the Lord of Sumer, Lord of the Air, Bringer of Civilization,

Ea, or Enki, Lord of the Ocean Depths, Lord of the Magic Arts, Lord of Earth, Benefactor of Mankind,

Ninhursag, the Lady of the Mountains, Mother of the gods,

Inanna, or Ishtar, the goddess of love and war,

Ninurta, the god of war,

Utu, or Shamash, the Sun god,

Nanna, or Sin, the Moon god,

Naba, Gula, Ningal, Adad, Nusku, Gibil, Mami, Oannes, Ishkur, Shala, Papsukal, Zu, Dumuzi, Nanshe, Ningursu, Ennuge, Tiamat, Ramman, Ninti, Nidaba, and on and on and on.

There was even an assembly of the gods, the members of which were called the Annunaki.

As beings endowed with intelligence and free will, the Sumerians were capable of rejecting the spurious claims of these beings, but they didn't. They willingly chose to forsake the only true God, the God of Creation, El Shaddai, and turned aside to follow the teachings of fallen spirits.

For these and other reasons, the Sumerians were destroyed by a just and holy God, along with the rest of humanity in the Great Flood. But the spiritual perpetrators of this falling away from God were not destroyed along with their human collaborators. Nor did they give up their desperate struggle to steal, kill, and destroy God's earthly and human creations. And now the humans were repopulating the Earth and were building cities, one of which was to have an immense impact on the subsequent course of human history.

But the Watchers remain; their work is not finished.

Their symbol is the all-seeing eye.

--⊸ CHAPTER FOUR ⊱--

Reza and Vashti

I t had been centuries since the descendants of Noah had
wandered onto the broad fertile plain of Shinar and there
established their homes, farms, and communities. Their principle
city, Babylon, had grown into a large, bustling city of broad avenues
lined with fine homes and busy shops, as well as narrow meandering
lanes where the less well to do struggled to eke out their lives.

Differences of skin color and facial features were evident among
the people, and the explanation for this was that these differences had
been passed down through the multi-ethnic wives of Noah's sons.

In addition to racial differences, social classes were already
forming in Babylonian society, partly due to the commandments of
their king and partly to the unequal mix of human characteristics
found in individuals — intelligent or dull, aggressive or passive,
honest or ruthless. The class at the bottom of society was the
wardum, the slaves and bonded servants. Slavery had been unknown
prior to Babylon's emergence, but now included conquered people,
captives, debtors, orphans, and individuals sold by traders. They
owned nothing and had no rights.

Above the *wardum* were the *mushkenum*, who were tenant
farmers living on land claimed by the king, and provided a portion
of their produce and animals to the royal household. Above the

mushkenum was the class of freedmen known as *awilum*. These were free farmers, craftsmen, and artisans who owned their own land, animals, and property. Above the *awilum*, and just below the royal family, were the aristocracy and the priests who were mainly privileged individuals with close ties to the king.

The success of *awilum* and *mushkenum* farmers in outlying areas had made possible the specialization of crafts and trades, which led to the concentration of people in towns, where goods could be sold and traded without having to travel long distances. Local artisans had developed a new technique of making multi-colored fire-glazed brick. This product was being used extensively for the large public buildings and structures that were being erected by the self-proclaimed king, Ninus. Behind his back, Ninus was already being called 'Nimrod', which meant 'the rebel', for he had strange and dangerous ideas in his head.

One local artisan, prominent in the making of fire-glazed brick, was a man named Zakir, who had a brick-making business on the recently renamed Marduk Avenue, where it intersected Enlil Street. This was a fortunate location for Zakir's business, for Marduk and Enlil was one of the busiest intersections in Babylon.

Zakir was assisted in his prospering business by his son Reza, a tall, handsome, black-haired young man of twenty years. Reza was responsible for overseeing twenty-two employees while his father worked with suppliers of the raw materials the business needed, as well as handling the contracting and finances.

Each day at lunchtime, Zakir and his son Reza would walk together through the marketplace on Zababa Street on their way home, where Zakir's wife, Ishabi, with the help of the family's servants, would have a sumptuous meal awaiting them. Reza eagerly looked forward to this walk through the market each day, but not because he anticipated a meal. And this beautiful spring day was no different. As he walked beside his father, his eyes strained ahead in search of the object of his desire. His heart began to pound as he and his father approached a certain fabric seller's stall.

Zakir smiled to himself as they neared the spot. "I remember pursuing Ishabi," he recalled.

Reza veered away from his father toward the fabric stall. As he approached, wide-eyed and panting, a woman working at the stall glanced up and saw him. She turned to the girl stacking rolls of cloth behind her and said, "Ahem, I think a certain young man would like to look at fabric. Will you help him, daughter?"

Now two hearts raced as a seventeen year old dark-haired beauty named Vashti whirled around and looked up expectantly with a smile breaking out across her lovely face. Their eyes met.

"Oh, Reza, it's you," she said, suddenly pretending to be unimpressed.

"Hello Vashti! How are you?" Reza said enthusiastically. "Father and I were just on our way home for lunch." Then, remembering his manners, Reza spoke to the girl's mother. "How are you Enna-nedu? Is everything well?"

"Quite well, Reza. How are things with you and your father's business?" the older woman replied.

"Quite well!" he declared in his most business-like manner. "The men are constructing a fourth kiln. We can't make bricks fast enough!"

"Very impressive!" said Enna-nedu. She then turned to other matters so her daughter could speak to her heart's desire.

"So Reza," Vashti said demurely, "will you be coming to the New

Moon Festival two days from now?" Reza just stared, moonstruck, with his mouth hanging open.

His father, Zakir, nudged him. "Go on boy, she's speaking to you!"

"Oh!" Reza stammered. "Yes, yes I will. Will you be there, Vashti?"

"Certainly!" the girl replied. "We can meet at the entrance to the Sacred Precinct at sunset, if you like," she added, teasingly.

Reza stood gasping, wordless. His father nudged him again.

"Yes, that would be great...at the entrance to the Sacred Precinct...at sunset," Reza repeated, as his father began to pull him away.

"I'll see you then, Vashti!" he called out as he bumped into a donkey that brayed angrily at him.

Vashti looked at her mother and giggled. Her mother smiled knowingly.

"Ah, life, and love, must have their way" the older, wiser woman murmured to herself. "And so must pain,"

Vashti gave one last look at Reza, who had turned to look back at her once more. He ran into two men who stood talking.

Begging the men's pardon, his father grabbed his son by the arm and jerked him along. Vashti and her mother threw their heads back and laughed loudly.

As father and son made their way through the crowded marketplace toward home, Reza spoke up urgently.

"Father... when?"

"It won't be long, son," Zakir replied assuringly. "I have spoken with Vashti's father, Samsu-iluna." Zakir allowed a tortuous pause before continuing. Reza stopped and stood still in the middle of the marketplace crowd, staring at his father.

"*And...?*" he cried out in anguish.

"He agrees to the match!" Zakir said, emotion welling up within him.

"*Heeeeyaaaa!*" shouted Reza, startling everyone around them. After jumping and spinning in the air, Reza ran to his father and threw his arms around him in gratitude.

Father and son strode through the market, their arms over each other's shoulders. Reza could not contain himself.

"*When*, Father?"

"One thing at a time, Reza," the older man said solemnly, "one thing at a time."

As Zakir and Reza walked homeward, they, and everyone else in Babylon were oblivious to an atmospheric event of unimaginable evil swirling above their very heads.

CHAPTER FIVE

The Vortex

The site for the city of Babylon had been chosen by King Ninus on the banks of the Euphrates River. The people wondered amongst themselves at the name he picked for the city, which meant 'Gate of the Gods'. "Curious name," the people muttered. They weren't sure which gods were being referred to since Ninus sometimes spoke of a deity called Baal, which meant Lord or Master. He was also frequently heard using this title along with the name Marduk, supposedly at his wife's prompting. Then there were all the other so-called 'gods' — Anu, Adad, Shamash, Ishtar, Tiamat, Ninurta, and a bewildering array of others, each with its own special personality and powers.

Little did the people understand the ominous link between the strategies of Ninus and those of the menacing conclave hovering above their growing, bustling city.

Invisible to their eyes, a dark revolving structure composed entirely of spirits whirled like a monstrous tornado in slow motion, stretching from a point just a stones' throw above the rooftops of Babylon and extending upwards and outwards into the sky.

In the midst of the swirling cloud was Chulgomet, in a central place of authority, and poised to address the assembly. At the proper moment he mentally shifted his thoughts to a resonance through which he could communicate with the storm of malignant beings that churned all around him, chanting in a deep undulating rhythm.

Chulgomet consciously raised his energy to a high level and began to 'speak', telepathically with his audience.

"Silence!" he thundered.

"I, Chulgomet, an Authority in the service of our Lord Lucifer, command your attention, all of you, from the highest rulers and dignitaries to the lowliest messengers. For I appear before you now having just come from the presence of our Lord. He has instructed me in great detail concerning the course that our strategy is to take with regard to the human creatures and our opposition to the Creator, whom we used to worship before we chose independence.

"You know well that the Creator's power far surpasses that of every one of us combined. You yourselves observed how he destroyed centuries of our labor simply by churning up the waters of the earth and sky. He could annihilate us by simply thinking the thought. But he will not!

"We are cast down, down into this battlefield, where he thinks that his justice and holiness will be vindicated by our own actions and by those of the human filth he seems to place so much importance on. He thinks that we will indict ourselves and thereby prove him holy."

At this the slowly spinning cloud of spirits began its low, sonorous chanting again. But Chulgomet was in a prideful mood.

"Silence!" he shouted. "We have business of the utmost importance to tend to! We will now review the progress we have made with the one called Ninus, whom the humans refer to as

Nimrod the rebel."

Chulgomet paused, his head tilted slightly upward, eyes closed, as he received telepathic information from one of his recording assistants. He then continued. "Very well. As you are aware, through the successful intervention of our Dominion Official, Jeramothe, we have inspired one of the human animals, Ninus, to dominate his fellows through intimidation and violence. He kills without mercy, and everyone who has stood up to him has been butchered like one of their ridiculous sin offerings. Jeramothe has succeeded in blinding him to the lesson passed down through his forebears concerning the crime of Cain, who murdered his brother Abel, as well as to God's destruction of the previous order of humans. Yes, the intentions and passions of Ninus coincide quite nicely with ours. He cooperates fully!"

Chulgomet added bitterly, "And this is all necessary now, Colleagues, for as you are aware, our freedom to interact directly with the humans has been restricted by the Creator. Therefore, our lord Lucifer has determined that our strategy shall be to entice humans to destroy themselves!"

Chulgomet resumed his discourse. "Colleagues, warfare and aggression among the humans have begun! Nimrod the rebel, will be known as a Hunter; not a hunter of animals, but a hunter of humans, a reaper of bodies and souls! And others will follow his example."

Chulgomet lowered his head and looked puzzled. "For reasons I cannot fathom, the Creator's ideal is that of a *Shepherd King*! Can you believe it? Can you understand it? A gentle Shepherd King who expends himself for the good of his flock! The information I have received is that this lunatic idea of God's — this Shepherd King — will figure, both humanly and otherwise, very largely in our future. *Our* ideal for the humans, therefore, is the Hunter of Men, who gratifies himself at the expense of his victims!

"We have already escalated, through the efforts of Jeramothe and his captain Gbatha, the use of weaponry, not only for hunting animals, but also for hunting and destroying humans! This bloody passion is driven by pride and the lust to exert one's will over others and to take what is theirs. We have excited this passion, this bloodlust, in Ninus and his followers. Some of the humans will now, under our influence, exert their wills to commandeer other humans for their own purposes. The masses will be led to slaughter their fellows, as they would *pigs,* without even knowing why!

"Do you see the beauty of it Colleagues? These repulsive fleshly beings, inexplicably gifted by God with free wills and the capacity to... aagh, *love,* will instead destroy each other for no good reason, other than the fact that we have driven them to it, in the very face of God who made them! And they are already doing this in complete disobedience to the laws and commandments of the Creator, passed down to them by that reprehensible Noah and his descendants."

At this, the beings in the swirling vortex resumed their chanting, this time communicating delight and approval. Chulgomet, puffed up with pride, continued.

"Quiet! Do you see how Ninus taxes the livelihood of the people to finance his aggression and his public works? It's all done to satisfy his pride and lust for power, the very things for which we have been cast down on this wilderness of a planet! From this time onward, the systems that men devise to govern themselves will be concerned with the shedding of innocent blood, the raising of ostentatious and unnecessary public works that benefit practically no one, and a crazed lust for power, all paid for with the toil, sweat, and suffering of ordinary citizens.

"Jeramothe and his cohorts have carried out their assignments expertly, uh, thus far." He cast a sidelong glance toward Jeramothe to stifle the arrogant gloating he was about to indulge in. Jeramothe snapped to attention as he spun past Chulgomet.

"But what we are accomplishing through Ninus, or Nimrod, as the people are now calling him, deals primarily with the physical domain of human existence. We must bear in mind that humans, as disgusting as they are, are more than just physical beings. Remember that their original forebear, Adam, was created in the spiritual image of God. That image was marred through disobedience, thanks to the timely and inspired intervention of Lord Lucifer! As a result, Adam's descendants carry the same tarnished spiritual image. We will have more to say about that later. But in order to thoroughly corrupt their hearts, the wellspring of their lives, we must drive them to spiritual rebellion!"

Chulgomet then sent forth a mental summons and a moment later a large, vile spirit appeared in front of him. Chulgomet presented the spirit to the entire assembly.

"Marduk, our colleague and a High Authority, will now provide us with an update on his progress with the wife of Nimrod the Rebel. She is called Semiramis. Our Lord Lucifer believes that the best way to draw Nimrod and his subjects into spiritual apostasy is through his wife. For contrary to God's command she enthusiastically seeks to make contact with spirits, not realizing, yet, that she is communicating with us.

"Henceforth," Chulgomet said, pausing for effect, "humans who make contact with us should always be rewarded with a sense of power. The energizing power that animates us can be channeled to them, in lesser degrees of course, but enough to energize and excite them. That will be all you need in most cases to attract and keep them!

"And now I present to you the esteemed Lord Marduk."

At this prompting, Marduk shifted his attention to the cloud of spirits whirling about him and began to communicate with them.

"Fellow conspirators against the Most High God" he began, sarcastically enunciating the words 'Most High God'.

"Lord Chulgomet has already informed you concerning the progress we have made in raising up a leader among the humans, a proud, vicious man who does not hesitate to shed blood to achieve his aims. Under the guidance of Jeramothe and his cohorts this man Ninus, also called Nimrod, has turned his back on God, nor does he show love — that repulsive word! — or compassion toward his fellow humans. He is our prototype for the human leaders to come, for he has cooperated with us fully and is now a hunter and destroyer of men, doing our work for us.

"Rejoice colleagues!" Marduk shouted. "For in the beginning God made man in his own image, but we have succeeded in re-making man in *our* image!"

At this, there was a spontaneous, deafening outburst of celebration from the swirling, living cloud that surrounded Marduk, who gazed about exultingly.

"As Lord Chulgomet has pointed out," he continued, "the corruption of the human race must take place not only in the physical realm but also in the spiritual realm. In fact, spiritual corruption is infinitely more important because eternity is involved. For as you are aware colleagues, these animals called humans are endowed with immortal souls."

At this there emerged a loud rumbling murmur of disapproval from within the vortex.

The former seraph angel Asmera, who excelled in his hatred of mankind, interrupted, "I share your sentiments colleagues; such a shabby, wasteful thing on the part of the Creator. But Marduk is correct, as you know. Or is it *Baal-Marduk* now? Very impressive that the humans address you as Lord Marduk! In any case, we must bear in mind that the destruction, degradation, and spiritual apostasy of the humans are the key elements in our war against our enemy, God — El Shaddai. By corrupting them we smite the Creator and confound his purposes, which appear to have the simpering emotion of *'love'* at their core."

"I will elaborate on this presently myself, Asmera," Chulgomet interjected sternly. "Your disrespect for protocol is disturbing. Confusion is part of our overall strategy, but not, I repeat, *not*, during a high conclave such as this! Continue, Lord Marduk."

Asmera shot a murderous glance at Chulgomet, who smiled back, reveling in his authority.

Marduk, frowning at the interruptions, began anew. "Colleagues, my cohorts and I have visited the weak-minded priests that the queen, Semiramis, has surrounded herself with, and have succeeded in channeling to them a corrupted version of God's creation. They call it the *Enuma Elish*, and in it we depict God in a most delightfully degraded fashion. You would be delighted to read it! I have also suggested to them the worship of myself, Marduk, as their patron god, per our Lord Lucifer's instructions.

"I am most pleased to report," he continued, "that we have seduced this woman, the queen, and have led her to worship and adore the sun, moon and planet Venus! She addresses the sun as Baal, which in their language means Lord, and she addresses Venus as Baalti, or Lady. Under our guidance she will publicly identify her husband Nimrod as 'Baal', the lord sun, and herself as 'Baalti', the goddess represented by Venus, and will require her subjects to do likewise, under pain of death. Think of it colleagues, enforced idolatry, under pain of death! It's beautiful!

"We find her easy to influence," Marduk continued. "She is vain and proud. Our kind of woman! We have carefully directed her in the use of her feminine charms to get her way and attract the lustful attention of men. Many females, young and old, are already following her manipulative example."

"Tonight we will visit her again. She was instructed previously to promote, through her husband Ninus, the building of a great tower, crowned with a temple, to honor and exalt us. For when they worship the sun and moon, planets and stars, they are worshipping us and our Lord Lucifer, the Bringer of Light.

"Yes colleagues," Marduk continued, "their sacrifices are unwittingly offered to us! But, as Lord Chulgomet has instructed us, part of our strategy lies in using a multiplicity of names. We cannot lead people to openly worship our Lord Lucifer; it must be done indirectly, under the guise of other names."

"Keep that in mind always when dealing with humans," Chulgomet admonished. "The more names the better, as it only increases confusion and hides the true identity of the one they are worshipping.

"Lord Marduk," Chulgomet concluded, "you and your cohorts have their orders. You will visit Queen Semiramis tonight in the inner chamber where she has placed an idol that bears your name and image. There you are to channel information to her in accordance with our Master's instructions.

"Oh, Lord Marduk, it may interest you to know that our Master, the Lord Lucifer himself, will accompany you tonight."

CHAPTER SIX

Semiramis and Marduk

Queen Semiramis awoke with a start, lying on the cold stone floor of the private inner chamber where she worshipped Marduk. She raised herself up on her elbows and glanced around frightened. She was drenched in sweat and felt a combination of nervous energy and lust, as though she had had one of her liaisons with Yasmah-adad, the handsome young soldier whose official duty was to guard the entrance to the queen's chambers. The king would have had Yasmah's head on a platter if he had known about the guard's relationship with the queen. But there was the idol of Marduk leering down at her with an evil grin, as though it were he who had just had Semiramis, for in truth he had.

Semiramis looked around her worship chamber and shivered as the experience she had just had swept over her in full force. She noticed the remains of an incense offering still smoldering in the bowl at Marduk's feet, and as she followed the thin wisp of smoke upwards, her gaze focused on the idol's face and she swooned as she realized that it closely matched the face of one of the beings in her vision.

Vision? No, it was more than that. Her body, mind, and soul told her that what had just happened to her was very, very real.

She remembered awakening in the night, hearing a voice

35

summoning her to her worship chamber. It was a still, yet insistent voice, not heard with the ears but rather felt, speaking directly to her understanding. She obeyed, sensing that something momentous was about to happen. Her snoring husband was oblivious as she slid out of their bed.

Tiptoeing down the dark stone corridor, she stopped suddenly, jolted by her conscience. It warned her of danger and urged her to turn immediately to God — the one true and only God — and to flee from the spirit Marduk who demanded worship that rightly belonged to God alone.

Semiramis' earthbound vision prevented her from seeing the fantastic multidimensional struggle that swirled around her. As mighty spirit beings clashed, a staggering and bewildering mystery revealed itself. For reasons known only to God himself, the struggle was determined by an act of will, not divine will or the will of spirit beings, but by human will. Omnipotence voluntarily stood aside and allowed the free will of a frail human being to decide the issue.

The queen paused, looked around, and shook her head as though pestered by a gnat, and continued down the hallway toward Marduk's chamber. The spiritual battle behind her subsided, and the forces involved withdrew, one side with somber resignation, the other exulting.

The queen groped her way to her worship chamber and fearfully stepped inside. A tangible presence beckoned her into the small, dark room. She instinctively knelt before the idol of Marduk, as was her custom, and began to worship.

A flash of dazzling light momentarily blinded her and she immediately found herself standing in the presence of two mighty beings of light, one much more powerful and arrogant than the other. The lesser of the two spoke first.

"I am Marduk, Lord of your city, Babylon. I am the living spirit behind the idol in your inner chamber. I have found your adoration to be most pleasing."

Semiramis, speechless, could only listen.

"You are greatly honored," he continued, "to be the chosen vessel of a new way of belief and worship, one which, with our guidance and direction, will cover the Earth. It will all be to the honor and glory of the one I introduce to you now. He will be known to you and your people as the Bringer of Light and Knowledge. But he shall also be Myrionymus, the One with Ten Thousand Names, for every tribe and nation under the sun will worship him by a name that we will give them through a chosen representative. The sun blazing in its glory shall be his emblem, for he brings light and life to mankind. He will now instruct you in the way he is to be worshipped and honored."

A great rush of terrifying excitement gripped Semiramis as the other being, indescribably beautiful, but at the same time, indescribably dangerous, loomed closer to her. He had a radiant face with blazing eyes. His mouth remained closed as he began to communicate with her telepathically. She stood rigid, held by his gaze, as his words reverberated in her mind.

"I began my existence as the model of perfection, full of wisdom and perfect in beauty, for thus I have been told. I was in Eden, the Garden of God; every precious stone adorned me. I was anointed as a Guardian Cherub, ordained by God. I was on the holy mount of God; I walked among the fiery stones. I was blameless in my ways from the day I was created until knowledge was found in me.

It was then I asserted myself by declaring before all of creation, 'I *will* ascend to heaven, I *will* exalt my throne above the stars of God; I *will* sit enthroned on the mount of assembly, on the utmost heights of the north. I *will* ascend above the tops of the clouds; *I will make myself like the Most High GOD!*

It is I who have brought wisdom, light, and knowledge to the inhabitants of earth. Knowledge that God would withhold from men, knowing that with it, they would become gods *like Him!* Since *he* withholds it *I* shall reveal it! Thus it is *I* who am worthy of praise and glory and honor! *I* shall be exalted among mankind!

And you, Semiramis, you and your husband, are my chosen vessels."

The mighty being, Lucifer, then overshadowed and enveloped Semiramis, who stood transfixed. She yielded herself to him in ecstasy.

Returning to the present, the queen raised herself from the cold stone floor and stood, quaking, to her feet.

"Sula!" she screamed. "Sulamith, where are you?"

Within moments a young teenage servant girl, sleep still in her eyes, fearfully peered into the candlelit chamber.

"Yes, Baalti, my Lady, I'm here!" she squeaked.

"Summon my priests — the *mashmashus*! All twelve of them!" shouted Semiramis.

"Now, my Lady?" questioned Sula, knowing that it was the middle of the night, and that the corrupt priests the queen surrounded herself with were prone to drunkenness and revelry.

"Did I say 'tomorrow' Sulamith? Get them now or I'll have your hide!" The girl shrieked and ran to carry out her orders.

Semiramis paused and took a deep breath, steadying herself.

Then looking down she noticed that her gown was undone, revealing her naked body beneath. Her hair was disheveled and she was still sweating profusely in spite of the chilled night air.

"I can't let them see the queen like this," she said to no one in particular, and stepped toward the doorway, which had just been hastily evacuated by her servant girl.

Semiramis stopped, turned, and instinctively rushed back to her idol. Realizing now that the idol of stone was a portal leading into the presence of a real being, a being of light and wisdom, she climbed upon the pedestal, and wrapping her arms around Marduk like she would a human lover, she placed her lips on the lips of stone. Then, leaning her head back she cried out lustfully,

"I know exactly what to do!"

CHAPTER SEVEN

The Mashmashus

Twelve yawning, hung-over priests, known as *mashmashus,* assembled clumsily in the queen's reception hall, rubbing their eyes, scratching their heads and looking rather comical. Some still wore tunics stained with spills from the previous evenings' carousing.

"Not quite the pompous, self-righteous windbags they normally are, strutting about the city like bantam roosters!" the queen mused.

In Nimrod and Semiramis' presence, however, it was a very different show they put on. Before the king and queen they were the very picture of fawning, obsequious 'yes men'.

Priests? From the time of Noah and the Great Flood until Ninus' founding of the City of Babylon, men had been under God's commandment to serve as the priests of their own households, preserving and transmitting God's revealed truths from one generation to the next. There was no other kind of priest. There was no other religious organization.

Under this arrangement everyone knew his or her place in the grand scheme of things, including their proper relations with other people and with God, who had made them for a special relationship with himself.

Everyone, great and small, knew that they had inherited a tendency to sin, or act contrary to God's will, as revealed in their consciences, and to thereby become alienated from the holy, righteous One who made them. They knew, further, that atonement for sin, and reconciliation with God, had to be through the sacrifice. For, as they had been instructed from childhood on, 'Apart from the shedding of blood there is no forgiveness of sins'. Without forgiveness of sins there was no fellowship with God, for God, who is absolutely pure, holy, and righteous cannot simply forgive sins with a wave of the hand, as a doting grandparent might, for to do so would contradict his own character. For this reason, as everyone was well aware, a sacrifice was required to satisfy the just punishment for sin. And since people, being human, would eventually sin again, another sacrifice, and another, and another was required to reconcile the repentant one with his Maker.

However, Ninus and Semiramis, in their pride and lust for power, gathered to themselves a group of easily corruptible men and established a priesthood through which they could reach into the homes, the hearts, and the purses of the people they ruled. The organization was clumsy and heavy-handed at first, much like Ninus' tax collectors, and people resented the new priestly caste and its attempts to control their spiritual, and temporal, lives.

But now Ninus was preoccupied with the conquest and subjugation of other tribes, and his queen, Semiramis, was aflame with Luciferic inspiration. She saw in the motley crew of priests before her a means, not just of controlling the people of Babylon, but of controlling and directing *the world* for the glory of the great and wise being of light who visited her, Marduk's lordly companion, the one called *Myrionymus*...the One with Ten Thousand Names!

Semiramis eyed the shuffling group of priests intently. "I have been visited by the great god and prince of this world!" she began.

The queen was gorgeously arrayed now. Her hair was brushed and adorned with a glittering tiara, studded with diamonds, her eyes and lips painted, her voluptuous body barely covered with a very revealing white gown girded at her hips with a gold chain.

Twelve pairs of hungry eyes were fastened on her as she stood proudly before them, reveling in their lustful attention.

"He has revealed his purposes and desires to me," she continued. "He is the most beautiful and wise of all creation, the greatest of all beings. He has brought wisdom and enlightenment to mankind and has shown me the way.

"As a people," she continued, "we once mistakenly directed our worship to One who withheld from us that which is good — the knowledge of our own godhood!

"He withholds from us what is good and instead requires us to grovel before him pleading for forgiveness. Why would he want that? It doesn't matter. That is over now, for I have been shown a better way!"

One of the priests, a local man named Nebu-shahash, fidgeted uncomfortably, having second thoughts about things. "But Baalti, my...my lady," he stammered, "we were raised with the knowledge that there is only one God, the God of all creation. There are other spirits, lesser beings than God, some good and some corrupt, but I can't get over the feeling that they are not to be worshipped. Our forefathers made *that* mistake before the Great Flood!"

Semiramis' eyes narrowed threateningly. She had heard this before, and was in no mood for it now. She began to move toward Nebu-shahash, with slow, deliberate, catlike steps. She reached behind her back, then brought her hand slowly forward, concealing a shiny object. She was prepared for such insubordination.

Nebu-shahash, unaware of his peril, glanced to either side looking for support from his fellows. They stood silently and stared straight ahead. He had brought this up before. He had been warned.

"If I may beg your pardon, Baalti," he continued, "It's a dangerous business, as it is, leading the people in the worship of these other beings, like this Anu that people now worship as the Creator and father of the gods. We have always known the Creator as El Shaddai, God Almighty. Then you told us that someone called Ishtar had revealed himself, uh, herself rather, to you as the goddess of love and procreation and...and war and bloodshed."

He shook his head, unable to make the connection between sex and violence.

"I've never felt comfortable with that," he continued, "or with this Marduk being who communicates with you in your inner chamber. Or, who is this Tiamat, a goddess that the people now believe causes confusion and chaos. Does it ever end Baalti? he whined. "Per your instructions we have added the name of yet another new god — Nebu — to our own names."

Unnoticed by Nebu-shahash, the other priests began shifting away from him, almost imperceptibly, on both sides. Oblivious, he continued.

"But this newest spirit that you say has now revealed itself to you, I fear, is none other than the great enemy of man, our adversary, the one who deceived Father Adam and Mother Eve to..."

Semiramis' hand struck like lightning.

A wicked gash across Nebu-shahash's neck spurted blood down

the front of the queen's gown as he sank to his knees wide-eyed, gasping and gurgling.

Semiramis coldly wiped her blade clean on his forehead, and to the stunned horror of the other priests, lifted her leg, and placing the sole of her foot on Nebu-shahash's face, shoved him over backwards onto the stone floor.

"Does anyone else share our poor Nebu-shahash's misgivings?" she murmured.

No one spoke.

CHAPTER EIGHT

Reza and the New Religion

Nimrod and Semiramis stood side by side on the marbled terrace of their palace, looking out over the great city they were building. A mighty wall was being constructed that would ultimately encircle the city.

"Wide enough to race four chariots side by side along the top of it!" the king boasted.

Broad avenues were being laid out by surveying crews, as were smaller streets and alleyways. On their immediate right ran the river Euphrates, on the far side of which construction was commencing on streets, walls, and temples. The city would straddle both sides of the river.

Looking south, they could see the temple of Shamash, where the baldheaded priests, the *mashmashus*, could be seen going about their duties, purifying the worship paraphernalia and tending the sacrificial fires. Closer to the royal couple, directly across from the temple of Shamash, an enormous square-shaped area had been cleared and graded, and construction was underway on a colossal *ziggurat,* a seven-tiered pyramid, the purpose of which had not been publicly revealed. Since stone was not readily available for construction purposes, Nimrod's public works projects were built with brick which was enameled with brightly colored glaze.

Semiramis, moved close to her husband, clasping his arm. "We are gods, my husband!"

"Uh, yesss" he replied, only half mockingly. "Right you are O' mighty Ishtar, goddess of war — and *love*! Is that not a contradiction my queen?"

He turned and faced her, taking her forcefully into his arms. Eye to eye now, he continued. "You have the people believing you, my lioness. You almost have *me* believing it too!"

At that moment a bell sounded outside the royal couple's chamber. Recognizing the sound, Ninus called out "Enter!" Moments later a bald eunuch appeared, wearing only the mid-thigh length skirt of the palace servants.

"My Lord Ninus," he said effeminately, "the generals await you in your war chamber."

"Call my armor bearer," commanded the King.

Far below the king's terrace, in the bustling avenues of Babylon, the young brick-maker Reza and his father, Zakir, stepped up to the door of a fine looking home on Ninurta Street. Zakir knocked while Reza shuffled in the dirt, rehearsing in his mind what he would say to Vashti when he was alone with her, assuming that would be permitted.

The door opened and a gregarious well-dressed man in an embroidered tunic appeared at the threshold. It was Samsu-iluna, Vashti's father, who now grinned and welcomed Zakir by extending his hand. The two men clasped each other's wrists in a masculine greeting. Then Samsu-iluna turned and faced Reza, whose eyes widened expectantly.

"And how is the young man who wants to marry my daughter?"

the older man boomed, pretending to be dreadfully serious.

"Um, quite well, sir. And you sir, are you well?" Reza replied nervously.

Samsu-iluna threw his head back and laughed loudly. But now, showing mercy, he became serious and extended his hand to Reza as he would to any of his own peers. Reza quickly took note of his future father-in-law's gesture and clasped wrists with him, as his own father had taught him.

Seized now with a feeling of love for the young man who would soon be his son-in-law and the father of his grandchildren, Samsu-iluna threw his arm around Reza's shoulders and gestured for him to enter his home.

Once inside, Samsu-iluna turned to Zakir and said, "So how goes the brick-making my friend? I hear you're expanding your business. That's good news!" While the two men talked, Reza peered about anxiously. He didn't care about business at this moment. He was young. It was spring. He was in love.

His love's mother, Enna-nedu, stepped into the entrance hall of the home to greet the visitors. She then directed Reza to follow her and left the older men to discuss the important upcoming plans that would unite their families.

Enna-nedu's home was laid out in a rectangular fashion with an open courtyard in the center, surrounded by a covered walkway. In the courtyard was a lush garden. The courtyard and garden were filled with exotic flowers, bushes, and trees. At the center of the garden was a pond and a fountain.

As they strolled through the house, Enna-nedu inquired politely about Reza's mother and sisters. When they reached one of the entrances to the interior courtyard and garden area, Enna-nedu smiled knowingly at the young man and said, "Perhaps you and Vashti would like to chat while I prepare refreshments."

Reza stared and said nothing.

"Go, young man!" Enna-nedu whispered sharply. "Vashti is in the garden! Shoo! Off with you!" she said, fluttering her hands in the air. Reza needed no further prompting.

As Enna-nedu turned to summon her kitchen servants, she glanced back once more and watched as the excited young man took off in pursuit of his love, her own beloved daughter, Vashti. Tears began to flow and the mother sobbed, wracked with intense feelings of joy, longing, and loss. She sensed that her daughter was no longer hers and was now entering life's premier rite of passage. Life and love would have their way, as would pain.

Reza found Vashti sitting by the pond in the center of the garden, dangling one bare foot delicately in the cool water and looking up at the clouds drifting slowly overhead as if she had no care in the world. But she knew who approached her now, and she had to gasp for breath.

"Vashti!"

"Reza!"

There was no pretension now.

Reza reached down with both hands. Vashti took hold of his hands and he helped her to her feet. A long moment passed as they looked into each other's faces. Then their lips met.

"No good will come of this, Samsu," Zakir said frowning and shaking his head worriedly. "This new religion goes against everything we've ever known about our God, El Shaddai." The two men were seated in Samsu's office where he managed the affairs of a prosperous fabric business.

Samsu-iluna nodded solemnly. "There is no god but the Nameless One, the one we know by his title — El Shaddai — the Almighty God. As for this Marduk and Ishtar and all the rest, they can be nothing but our spiritual enemies...demons!" Samsu turned his head and spat.

"Ninus and Semiramis and their so-called priesthood, that sleazy high priest and his *mashmashus*, are leading us down a road to destruction!" Zakir said in stunned amazement.

Suddenly, realizing that they were speaking treason, both men glanced toward the window that opened to the street to make sure no unfriendly ears were listening.

Samsu-iluna grew very serious, "Zakir, old friend, the most unsettling thing of all is they are forcing the people to worship these gods who are not gods at all."

"That's true, that's true," Zakir agreed. "My wife, Ishabi, tells me that the meat in the marketplace is being consecrated to these ... these ... demon-gods of theirs before being put up for sale. How can we eat meat that has been defiled in this way?"

"And now they are taxing us to support their corrupt priest-hood!" complained Samsu. "Think of it Zakir, our hard-earned money going to those lazy, drug-addled *mashmashus*! What next?"

Just then, a visibly shaken Reza appeared in the doorway. Looking down dejectedly, he said, "I'm ready to go when you are, Father."

"Alright Reza, I think Samsu and I are finished here," replied Zakir.

Once outside Zakir turned to his son.

"What happened in there Reza? Did you and Vashti have an

argument before you are even married?" he said laughingly.

"Something like that," Reza mumbled. "I just told her about a decision I made recently. She tried to talk me out of it, then ran crying to her room. Her mother wouldn't let me go to her. It's something I haven't told anyone about, not even you, Father."

"Sounds serious," replied his father.

"I've been meeting with the priests of Marduk, Father. They think I have great potential. They've shared some of their secrets with me. It's really quite amazing, what they know. They know the secrets of the universe!"

Zakir, filled with a sudden dread, struggled to breath.

"They want me to join their priesthood" Reza said excitedly. "I've accepted!"

A strong hand grabbed Reza by the shoulder and spun him around. Before he could respond, his father's fist landed directly in the center of Reza's face. Looking up from the ground, Reza saw his father standing over him, his fists clenched, with a look of shock, rage, and disbelief on his contorted face.

"I am of age, Father!" Reza shouted. "I make my own decisions!"

CHAPTER NINE

War Strategy

Ninus, the King of Babylon, now clad in his armor, stepped into a spacious, cedar-paneled room where his generals awaited him anxiously. He peered around the room and let his gaze rest momentarily on each man seated at the rectangular wooden table, riveting the attention of each one.

However, the king and his generals were oblivious to the fact that there were other beings in the room. For behind each man was a powerful spirit, under direct orders from the High Authority Chulgomet to sway and influence the humans toward destruction and bloodshed.

Behind and around Ninus, moving in and out of him at will, was the spirit lord Marduk, exulting in his task.

Ninus addressed his generals by name, "Nebu-zaradan, Nebu-sarsekim, Nergal-shahrezer, Nebu-shazdan: as you are aware, Generals, the Sharukka tribe, whose chief village of Dur Sharukkin is located one hundred and eighty miles north of us on the Tigris River, has chosen to rebel against my authority!" He glanced around at his officers incredulously.

"Imagine that," he added humorously, "rebelling against Ninus the Rebel!" A chuckle went around the room.

The king continued, "They not only reject my authority, but

they still cling to the old God of Noah and Father Adam. They reject Lord Shamash, the sun, as well as Anu, the Creator. We have ordered them to worship Marduk and Ishtar, but they stubbornly refuse. To make matters even worse, they refuse to pay the tribute and taxes I have levied on them."

"Finally," Ninus said exasperated, "those fools are charging far too much for the coal and oil products that come from the pits near their villages. We must have these products to make the enameled bricks for our public works, temples, and monuments. They are draining our treasury!" the king ranted.

The spirits in the room merged with their appointed victims. Ninus was inflamed by the spirit now in possession of him.

"As you know, Generals, the people are unaccustomed to violence. They have always been able to settle disputes peaceably, even when it meant the separation of tribes or clans moving away from each other and settling in other lands. This makes our task an easy one. For months the ironworkers and smiths of Babylon have been making weapons and armaments of war. My assistant, Arioch, will now give his report on our preparations.

"My Lord the King, and Generals," the king's administrator began, "according to reports from the king's chief-of-arms, Lugal-zagesi, we have sixteen hundred footmen, outfitted with protective armor, helmets, shields, spears, and swords. We have four hundred archers, similarly clad with protective gear. We have outfitted two hundred mounted lancers. Finally, one hundred and forty chariots have been prepared and outfitted with horses. The workers have been instructed, per your orders, O King, to fashion blades to be fitted to the hubs of the chariots. Whoever manages to step clear of the horses will be cut to ribbons!"

Arioch continued, "Mule-drawn carts are being loaded with food, utensils, and other provisions. Each cart will be manned by a cook and an assistant. Astrologers, physicians, and priests will accompany the troops. Per the king's orders, all personnel, including the king himself and the generals, will sleep on the ground and will take their meals along with the common soldiers."

The king commended his assistant, "Well done Arioch."

As Arioch withdrew, Ninus stood and leaned forward, his fists on the table, eyes narrowed. "I have been visited by Marduk, Generals," he began.

Marduk, hearing his own name, cast a leering grin at his fellow spirits.

The king continued, "He has revealed to me the strategy we shall follow henceforth in our warfare. Listen very closely Generals, for your own lives and families depend on how well you obey these instructions!

"We have, first of all, a clear and obtainable objective — the complete destruction of the Sharukka and their principle city, Dur Sharukkin. Not one person, not even babies at their mother's breasts, are to be left alive! Their homes are to be burned, their possessions and animals confiscated. Next, we have reliable information from our spies and scouts concerning the ability of the Sharukka to respond to our forces. At this moment, incredibly, they do not believe violence to be an option at our disposal. Apparently, they think that their worthless lives are of great value to their God, this, this God who supposedly created everything, this God of Father Noah! They will soon find out how much this God loves them!"

This brought a ripple of agreeable laughter to those seated around the table, as it did to the spirits hovering in and around them.

"As you have just heard from Arioch," Ninus continued, "our logistics and supply lines are designed to keep our troops fed and outfitted. And there are to be no women on this expedition!" the king suddenly shouted, slamming his fist on the table. The generals jumped in their seats. "Like men of war, we will, all of us — generals as well as foot soldiers — sleep on the ground, rain or shine!

"Now then, we have discussed our objective and logistics. Next, as we approach Dur Sharukkin our troops are to be divided and set in offensive positions forming a perimeter around the city."

Ninus suddenly stiffened as Marduk exerted focused energy to the king's willing mind.

"A strategic penetration of forces..." he said, barely able to conceal the trembling, nervous excitement that shook him.

"A strategic penetration of forces will take place," he repeated, "followed by a backup force that will widen the breach created by the initial thrust. Divide and destroy. *Divide and destroy!* We will take offensive action, giving us control over the place and timing of the conflict. We will strike when they least expect it. This will give us the element of surprise. We will be upon them before they know what is happening, and then it will be too late!"

Ninus' face was red, his heart pounding, energized with evil from without, combined with evil from within; a fallen human cooperating fully with fallen spirit, functioning together as one, in open defiance of the God who made them both.

"Finally, Generals," he concluded, gasping for breath, "our attack will be so sudden, so bloody, so overwhelming, so devastating, that word of it will spread like fire! We will be an absolute terror to all who hear! No one will dare resist us!"

The king suddenly stood erect, and staring into space,

announced — as though the information had just come to him, for indeed it *had* — "My subjects have taken to calling me Nimrod, which, as you know, means 'the Rebel.' I do not object to this name, Generals; it suits me well, for a rebel I am indeed! Let God do something about it, if he is able!

"Muster the troops at my command!" Nimrod concluded. "Dismissed!"

CHAPTER TEN

The New Occultism

Incense clouded the air in the king's war chamber as another kind of war strategy was about to unfold. Statues of Ishtar and Marduk were positioned on either side of the ornately carved royal chair at the head of the massive table. Seated around the table were twelve white-robed priests, including a newcomer, who was procured to replace the hapless Nebu-shahash.

There could now be no doubt in the men's minds that their very lives — not to mention the lives of their families — depended on their enthusiastic cooperation with Queen Semiramis. Not that they were unwitting stooges; for they themselves had experienced the ecstatic and terrifying excitement of coming into contact with the beings the queen called 'spirit masters'. There *was* hidden knowledge to be learned from them, knowledge to which the masses had no access. All that these beings, these ascended masters, required was to worship them.

But little could they have dreamed that they were about to be initiated into something so profound that it would guide the course of human events the world over.

They knew that something important was going to happen that night for the queen's explicit instructions were for the priests to assemble in the king's war chamber and she would meet them there at midnight.

It certainly did not put them at ease to be ushered into the darkened war chamber, lit only by incense burners on bronze stands, and find images of Marduk and Ishtar leering at them through the haze.

But Marduk and Ishtar themselves were present too, along with a legion of spirits.

Chulgomet led the delegation to oversee the imparting of the methods and rituals the humans were to use to approach and worship their unseen masters. Thousands of spirit beings thronged the war chamber in Nimrod and Semiramis' palace that night, moving freely, multidimensionally, in, around, and through the twelve priests seated at the table.

The priests fidgeted uncomfortably in their seats, experiencing a combination of dread mixed with tense excitement. From somewhere unseen, a slow, melodic drumbeat began to sound. As the pace picked up, so did the heartbeats of the twelve nervous priests.

Suddenly, without warning, there was a bright, burning flash in each incense burner, as though an invisible hand had thrown in a magical combustible material.

Then *she* entered.

What devilry was *this*?

The stunned priests could only stare aghast. Was this the queen?

A sultry female figure dressed in a black gown reaching to the floor entered the chamber and slowly glided across the smoke-filled room as though floating, and reaching the head of the table, came to a stop. After a long tense pause the apparition slowly raised its dark, turbaned head.

Frantic thoughts shot through the priest's minds, 'Is it the queen? Who is it? *What* is it?'

A dark-eyed woman lifted her gaze. It appeared to the mesmerized priests that the woman was opening and closing her eyes, first one eye then the other. But still her eyes remained open. As their vision recovered after the flash in the incense burners, the priests could see that the woman had an eye painted on each eyelid, giving the appearance of open eyes whether the eyelids were actually opened or closed.

She wore glittering silver makeup on her face, and bore an intricately painted sun on her right cheek, the moon on her left cheek. Her fingernails were long and painted black. The black turban on her head was fitted with a silver band, upon which was emblazoned a series of red broken cross figures. These represented the sun worship, and would be known to later generations as *swastikas*.

Filled with dread, their stomachs churning, the priests stared openmouthed.

The apparition spoke. "I have been alive forever," she began. "Before the world was created I was with the ascended masters of power, knowledge, and light. Since the creation of the world I have been countless things — a horse, a mouse, an aquatic insect, a tree, a man, a flower of the field. The cosmic energy that suffuses the universe flows through me. It is my task to set forth for humanity the illumined path to self-knowledge and godhood!"

The priests sat riveted, awaiting the revelation. They had tasted of these things themselves, and knew that Semiramis had a special gift, a special relationship with the spirit guides they had come to know. She had power. They had experienced it. They wanted more.

"The masses of people are cattle —*useless eaters!*" she ranted.

Yes, it *was* the queen.

"But we need them!" she continued. "We can draw energy, power, and worship from them!

"Some of us were destined to rise above them. We are the ones who have found the illuminated path, the way to knowledge, power, and godhood! Only the chosen few are worthy, those who are courageous, willing and able to, by their own hand, sever the cords that bind them to the earth, to ignorance!

"Listen to me carefully and I will reveal to you secret knowledge. You will experience power that you never thought possible! But this knowledge is not for everyone. Only the few. Only the worthy. Only those who have proved themselves through initiation!

"You will be among the first to be initiated into the way of power. But you must know," she said, boring holes into each priest with her eyes, "that if you reveal these secrets carelessly..."

The queen was now gliding around the table, letting her sharp fingernails scratch lightly across the back of each man's neck, sending icy shivers down each spine.

"... if you reveal these secrets openly... publicly... foolishly, you will suffer for it. You will never see your loved ones again. You, and they, will be disemboweled, and your throats slit from ear to ear. You will drown in your own blood.

"It won't end there," she continued menacingly. "The spirit lords, the ascended masters, who share the secret knowledge with us will have possession of your souls. There are no words in human speech that adequately describe what *they* will do with you — for all eternity!"

There was no movement in the room. The only sound was a

barely discernible gasping for breath, as twelve men struggled for air in the incense-laden chamber. They had witnessed the queen's cold-blooded murder of Nebu-shahash. If she was capable of such a deed, what could they expect from the spirit lords when betrayed by a trusted human?

Each man was filled with a silent dread that constricted his throat and made breathing almost impossible. There was no turning back now. They had seen too much. They had touched the flame.

It was real. The power was real. The Ascended Masters were real. But where would it all lead?

The black robed sorceress began again in earnest. "The masses are like beasts. They are not able to comprehend the secret knowledge, the power. They believe the spirits we worship to be somehow evil, malignant, harmful. If we tell them what we are doing they will not understand. They will be afraid and try to stop us, even by taking our lives.

"For this reason secrecy is essential. The truth is whatever suits our purposes. The goal justifies the methods of obtaining it.

"Here is what you must do," Semiramis said, leaning forward with her hands on the table. "Listen carefully! You are to maintain two kinds of ritual and ceremony. For the masses you will conduct an outward *exoteric* form of worship consisting of pomp and pageantry, forms and ceremonies, gorgeous robes and jewels, feast days, holy days, things to please the eye, the stomach, the emotions, things that will entertain the useless eaters! You will make idols they can see, touch, and adore. They will direct their love and their life energy to these idols, not realizing that the ascended masters stand behind them approvingly.

"Entice them with incense and candles," she continued, "with holy fires and holy water. Console them with fables. Make them drunk with wine. Above all else, establish yourselves and the priests you ordain as intermediaries between the people and the gods. Assert your right, indeed the necessity, of your presence to officiate at all of the peoples' life events such as births, deaths, marriages, planting and harvest times, and so on. Teach them that your absence from these normal human events will result in the direst consequences. This will give you control over their lives and keep them dependent on you. Of course," she sneered, "you must charge a fee for all of the services you provide!"

Semiramis paused until her priests became uncomfortable and fidgeted in their seats. Then she slowly enunciated her next statements.

"Keep ... the people ... in darkness.

"Keep them ... ignorant."

The queen seemed to be hovering above the floor, unnaturally tall. Her eyes seemed to be glowing.

She continued, "But these external rituals and symbols will be smoke and mirrors covering deeper spiritual realities of which the masses will know next to nothing. For unknown to the stupefied beasts who have gone home to their hovels and their mindless, animalistic tasks, there will be another form of worship, a hidden, *esoteric* ritual, with mysteries that plunge into the deeper realities! I'm referring to the way that leads to our godhood! But since the masses are unable to grasp these truths we will develop signs and symbols, the true meanings of which will only be known to us.

"We will make use of the sacred geometry developed by our architects and astrologers to design structures and monuments that serve our purposes and channel the cosmic energies that are all around us. The symbols will have no deep meaning to the masses but will mean much to those who are initiated. We and our followers will communicate with each other through these symbols. Differences of language will not be an obstacle to our occult communication.

"The great ones, the spirit masters, have revealed these symbols and their meanings as the appointed ways of approaching them, to honor and worship them, yes, to make a vital connection with them!" Semiramis exulted. "The unwitting crowds will bow before the symbols we display publicly, not knowing that they are bowing to unseen spirits!

"Ours shall become a worldwide brotherhood!" she said. "And our ultimate purpose is threefold. First, to exalt Lucifer, the Bearer of Light! His symbol for all time is to be the sun, blazing in its glory! Those who worship the sun, worship Lord Lucifer. But his name is never to be used openly. He will be known the world over by ten thousand names, spoken by people who do not truly know whom it is they are adoring!

"Our second great purpose is made possible by the first. We, the initiates of the secret knowledge, shall exalt ourselves, and by the strength of our own wills we shall seize knowledge and power and make ourselves gods!

"Finally," said the queen, licking her lips, "through the unlimited power of the ascended masters we will establish a celestial kingdom, a spiritual temple, composed entirely of the souls of men and women, boys and girls."

Twelve grinning, sweating priests jumped to their feet and shouted approvingly, as multitudes of rebel spirits joined in the chorus.

Queen Semiramis, energized by a force she had now learned to tap into at will, leaned forward again and said to her co-conspirators, "I will now tell you how all this is to be accomplished!"

CHAPTER ELEVEN

Spiritual Warfare

The whirling spirit vortex over Babylon seethed with expectant energy. Chulgomet was about to deliver an oration on what could possibly be the most important piece of strategy in the rebellious angels' entire warfare against the Creator.

Chulgomet and the other Authorities and Dignitaries, as well as lower level spirits, knew something about God that they considered to be a weakness. This weakness involved a feeling, an emanation, a force, that flows outward from one sentient being to another; something the Creator desired, above all else, to convey to his created beings, both spirit and human, and that those beings would in turn express toward him — by their own choice — without compulsion, without coercion, as an act of their own free wills.

This thing would be most inadequately expressed by the human word 'love'.

Love would be the sword with which the rebel Lucifer would smite the Creator!

Love was God's only weakness.

Chulgomet raised his hand and mentally projected a telepathic command to the cloud of spirits swirling around him.

"Silence Colleagues! Give me your undivided attention!" Chulgomet paused impatiently until he was satisfied every spirit was attentive.

"The moment has come," he began solemnly, "to discuss among the Rulers, Authorities, and Powers of the heavenly realms, the central mystery of the Creator's plan for humanity. As you know, we have been cast down to this mudspeck called Earth, imprisoned within its meager atmosphere, to languish with but a scant trace of our original power. We have been punished because we desired independence and power. But we can strike the Creator through his miserable human creation! The way to accomplish this, as before, is to deceive them into worshipping and following *us* instead of God. Pay attention and I will share with you the Lord Lucifer's plan!"

Time stood still as Chulgomet laid out Satan's master's plan to corrupt and deceive humanity.

"It is a great mystery, as you know Colleagues," Chulgomet continued, "but there dwells within the transcendent majesty of the Godhead, a multiple manifestation of personality; three personalities, to be precise. We do not understand it, but it has always been thus. It was this way when *we* were created countless eons ago — according to the way humans reckon time. We know it to be part of a grand design that awaits its full revelation. But here is what we do know: God created the humans in his own spiritual image, with glorified physical bodies. Their purpose, originally, was to love God and be loved by him! Fortunately, however, our master Lucifer succeeded in enticing them into disobedience. The Creator's image within them thus became marred and they became gross physical creatures. They lost their blessed state and became outcasts, hiding from God and doomed to toil, suffering and death!"

At this, a murmur of approval rumbled throughout the vortex.

"But to our dismay," Chulgomet continued, "the Creator is not finished with them. He has a plan, and according to our intelligence sources it goes something like this: In God's timing, he will raise up a people for himself — an ethnic group, a tribe, a *chosen people*. This will occur not far from the site of the garden in Eden where our Lord Lucifer deceived the prototype humans, Adam and Eve. The Creator's purpose in a chosen people is to create a gene pool from which will arise one born of a woman, who will supposedly bruise Lord Lucifer's head, whatever that means!"

Chulgomet sneered, "We think it an idle boast!

"Be that as it may," he continued, "this tribe will come to be called the Habiru, the Hebrews — 'the ones who passed through the waters'. God will do astonishing things in the presence of these Hebrews, but their lot is to stray from their God, and for that he must judge them.

"The secret," Chulgomet raised his voice for emphasis, "is to lure them into worshiping our own colleagues who will pose as the gods of the surrounding peoples and nations. This will result in shame, dishonor, and alienation from the Creator. Because of his holiness and justice he will have to withdraw his blessings from his own people, the apple of his eye. Thus we strike him again!

"But Colleagues, do not rejoice!" Chulgomet quickly added. "For this is only the first phase of God's greater plan. Once it is established that man cannot, in his own strength, measure up to God's standards of righteousness and holiness, ...oh I, I almost cannot bring myself to repeat this. I could not if Lord Lucifer had not required me to say it!"

The vortex slowed almost to a stop as its energy level subsided, awaiting Chulgomet's conclusion.

"Colleagues, you will not believe this!" Chulgomet ranted in exasperation, scarcely able to believe his own words. "Having proved that man cannot save himself, the Creator's plan is to provide mankind with a Savior! ... a Messiah! ... a Christ — the Anointed One! He will be born to a virgin woman and will, in himself, meet all the requirements of God's righteousness and holiness. He will then be delivered up as a living sacrifice for the sins of humanity, and whoever accepts this gift, through simple childlike faith, will become identified with this Savior in his death and resurrection and will thus become reconciled with the Creator, whom they will call their *Father!*"

The energy level in the vortex exploded with the rage of multitudes of spirits as they shouted their opposition to the Creator's plan of redemption for the humans.

Chulgomet raised his own energy level to a feverish pitch and shouted for order. Protocol spirits, stationed at intervals throughout the vortex, struggled to restore a semblance of order to the proceedings.

Chulgomet paused, striving to maintain his poise. He then resumed, nervously, knowing that the real outburst soon awaited him.

"You haven't heard the worst Colleagues." Chulgomet looked around anxiously, knowing that even in his high position as an Authority of the Hierarchy, a crowd of powerful beings like these could become menacing.

"As I have pointed out," he continued, "the Creator manifests a three-fold character. We do not understand this. But of these three personalities — shall we say *persons*? — one will leave his place of transcendent majesty in the Godhead and will be known as 'Immanuel' which means 'God with us', for indeed, this Savior — this Messiah — will be the radiance of God and the exact representation of his being!

"Yes, Colleagues," Chulgomet knew he now had little time to complete what he had to say. "It is the Creator's will to become one of them, so he can identify with them, and they with him! And through faith in this, this *God/Man*, humans will be indwelt by God's very spirit! They will become adopted as his children with rights of inheritance, an inheritance, both earthly and heavenly!

"Colleagues," Chulgomet added nervously, "this worldwide body of believers will be known as the Messiah's *bride!*"

Chulgomet felt the force of a blast strike him, even as he escaped into another dimension to avoid the onslaught. After recovering, and allowing time for the outrage to subside, he stepped back into the vortex.

"Colleagues, silence!" Chulgomet tried to reassert himself before the assembly, shamefully aware that he had just shown himself a coward.

"The battle has been joined! We will assault the human lineage of the Messiah at every point. We will be confronted by the Creator's warring angels, those fools who refuse to assert their godhood along with us! And Colleagues, do not dare to think that our Lord Lucifer is a fool with no plan or strategy to pursue in these matters. For confusion and deception are the key weapons in our arsenal!

"You have now heard," Chulgomet cried out, "of God's plan of redemption for humanity; how these revolting, wretched, walking jars of clay are to be temples of God's indwelling spirit!

"Well," Chulgomet added, "it is our sworn purpose to spread over all the earth a false and corrupted version of the Creator's plan of redemption, and we will accomplish this *before* he can carry out his own plan!

"You will see, Colleagues," Chulgomet concluded, "the humans will worship us, and our Lord Lucifer, the Bearer of Light!"

CHAPTER TWELVE

Ninus Rebuked

After the Great Flood the Sharukka tribe, whose adopted name meant 'righteous ruler', in honor of the great God of heaven, wandered down from the mountains and settled along the upper reaches of the Tigris River some one hundred and eighty miles north of Babylon. The Babylonians knew this region as Subartu.

The tribe's central village, Dur Sharukkin — 'the place of the righteous ruler' — numbered some 3000 inhabitants. It was governed by a council of elders, presided over by an *ensi*, or chieftain, named Shar-kalisharri, a wise and godly man.

The Sharukka prospered in the lands watered by the Tigris. The people cultivated wheat, barley, rye, corn, millet, and other cereals and grains. Their orchards grew apples, pears, figs, olives, almonds, plums, and many other delectables. They also raised horses, goats, sheep, donkeys, and camels.

The Sharukka held fast to the original religious traditions handed down by Father Adam and Mother Eve, to Noah, and then to his descendants. To the Sharukka there was one God, the God of Adam and Noah, the Creator of everything that exists, and to whom alone worship was due.

There was a stone altar on a prominent hilltop just outside of town, made with uncut stones, per the instructions of Father Noah.

There the elders of the tribe made the sacrifices for sin, consisting of the shedding of an animals' blood, followed by the sacrifice of burnt offerings. The sacrifices and rituals were performed by the elders and by men in their homes because there was no other priesthood.

The people of Dur Sharukkin also reverently obeyed the rules handed down from Noah concerning food. They observed the prohibitions on the consumption of an animal's blood and the eating of an animal that had been strangled. They were not to eat food that had been sacrificed to a false god, for they knew that behind every idol was a rebellious spirit. They obeyed the command to eat only those land animals with split hooves that chewed the cud, and to eat only water creatures that had fins and scales. They were permitted to consume many types of birds, but not the owl, eagle, vulture, raven, gull, stork, heron, or bat.

The tradition remained strong with the people of Dur Sharukkin that God, known as El Shaddai — God Almighty — was a loving God, but holy and just, and who sternly judged and punished spiritual adultery. He did so for it was the great mystery of God to endow each human and spirit with a free will, and although it was his loving desire that all obey him and attain eternal life, he did not force the issue. The Creator's existence was manifested in the creation itself as well as in each person's conscience. Therefore, every soul was without excuse. But free will was to remain free will. Thus ensued another mystery of God — his heartbreak over the wrong choices of his children.

The Sharukka knew that when a person died, it was decreed that he stand before God to give an account of his life. This instilled in the Sharukka a sense of worshipful awe that the people knew as the fear of God. This was not terror, but something more akin to the sense of wonderment, exhilaration, and helplessness that one experiences when gazing at the wonders and power of nature, and realizing that the One who created those wonders also held the destiny of each soul.

Needless to say, the Sharukka were greatly alarmed at the resurging paganism creeping up from the south, from Babylon; the very paganism that was so cataclysmically judged by God in the Great Flood. Messengers from Babylon had solemnly delivered the orders from Ninus, the King of Babylon, that the people of Subartu, including Dur Sharukkin, were to begin worshipping a pantheon of gods — Anu, Enlil, Ea, Marduk, Ishtar, Sin, Nergal, Ninurta, Adad, and the rest.

The Sharukka chieftain, Shar-kalisharri, patiently rebuked the messengers of the king, reminding them of the one true God of all, who destroyed mankind for its previous abandonment of him for following other gods, who were in fact not gods but fallen spirits. Having heard of the rampant immorality of Babylon, Shar-kalisharri also rebuked the king's messengers, instructing them that the dishonoring of one's body sexually was an especially grievous affront to a holy and righteous God. The messengers were kindly treated, but they returned to their king with an answer that greatly displeased him.

Enraged at this rebuke, Ninus had his palace sculptors prepare an image of Marduk and sent it to Dur Sharukkin with an imperial order to worship the idol, upon pain of death. The Sharukka were also ordered to immediately construct a temple for the idol, at their own expense, and institute a priesthood. These things the Sharukka firmly rejected. As a graphic lesson for the people, the elders of Dur Sharukkin set up the idol of Marduk at the edge of the town dump, which always smoldered with burning refuse. The town's people were summoned there en masse. At Shar-kalisharri's command, two stout young men swung large hammers and smashed the idol to pieces. The news of this event made its way quickly to Babylon.

As punishment the king imposed an annual levy on Dur Sharukkin of 500 pounds of silver and 250 pounds of gold — an impossible amount to raise! He also issued an order conscripting all Sharukka males between the ages of 16 and 30 to perform two years of military service for the king, and to be quartered at Babylon. These outrages were also rejected by the Sharukka.

But the king had something else on his mind. For the region of Subartu was abounding in a substance called bitumen, which served many useful purposes. The black, sticky substance welled up from underground and the Sharukka had discovered that when the bituminous sands were mixed with boiling water, the bitumen rose to the surface while the sand settled to the bottom. The bitumen, thus obtained, when further refined, could be used as an oil for heating, while in its dried form, as a soft coal, it could be used for cooking.

From bitumen, the Sharukka also produced a glue-like substance with many uses, as well as asphalts, which were useful for paving and construction. Finally, the people had learned to make paints and enamels from bitumen products that were used by the brick-makers and artisans of Babylon to make gorgeously colored enameled bricks, which Ninus desired for the massive public works under way in Babylon. The purchase of the enormous quantities of enamel he required was a drain on the imperial treasury.

That could be remedied.

A ten-day forced march brought Ninus and his troops into the precincts of Subartu. One morning as the sun rose the King stepped out of his tent and glanced around. His men were seated on the ground in their divisions eating breakfast. Each division had a banner emblazoned with the *mu-shushu*, the 'raging red dragon' of Marduk, fluttering ominously in the early morning sun. Ninus summoned his aide and said, "Tell the diviners to get ready."

While he waited for the astrologers and soothsayers, Ninus knelt down and stared into the distance, visualizing the destruction of Dur Sharukkin. While thoughts of death and mayhem filled his mind, the spirit Marduk hovered in and around the king, enflaming his violent passions. Soon, the aide returned and said, "Come my Lord, the diviners are waiting for you!"

Ninus approached a circle of men standing in the open desert. All eyes were on the chief diviner, called the *baru*. The bald-headed *baru*, grasping a large chicken, slit its neck with a ceremonial knife, then set the bird in the center of a pentagram — a five pointed star within a circle — drawn on the ground and marked with the signs of the zodiac and the gods. The hapless creature began to thrash about wildly — falling, standing, lurching one way then another — before collapsing in a fit of spastic contortions.

The *baru* and his colleagues leaned forward, eyes squinting as they carefully noted the bird's every movement. Behind them, equally intent, were the king and his advisors. Ninus shuffled in the sand nervously and cast a questioning glance at the *baru*.

"Well?" Ninus asked impatiently. "Does it bode well?"

"Excellent, my Lord!" the *baru* replied, clasping his white robe at the neck to ward off the early morning chill. "The creature's first reaction was a thrusting of the head skyward, looking to Enlil, Lord of the Air, Counselor to the gods, and Possessor of the Tablet of Destiny, by which the fates of men and gods are decreed. Then, not once, but thrice it bowed before the symbol of the god of war. With it's last steps — seven steps to be precise — it turned, and strode purposely to the symbol of the Sun God Shamash, Lord of Justice. The *baru* continued excitedly. "The number three signifies perfection, my lord, while the number seven indicates completion. Your war plans are perfect according to the gods, and will be carried out to perfect completion."

The *baru* now folded his hands to his chest, and looking skyward, continued, "Last night, O' King, the seers and I observed a most fortunate omen! The red planet of Marduk appeared in his glory, in close proximity to Nanna-Sin, the moon. Most auspicious!" he said gleefully, with spittle drooling down his chin. "Yes! The gods are honored! They look on you with favor!"

Then, at a nod from the *baru*, a young priest — a *mashmashu* — stepped forward and deftly skewered the chicken with his knife and opened up its belly. Reaching inside, he located the chicken's liver, and cutting it loose, brought it to the *baru*. The *baru* dropped to his knees, and accepting the liver in his two open palms, pressed it to his lips and then to his forehead and invoked the gods Ea and Enlil for guidance. He then gazed intently at the bloody organ and gently stroked it with his fingertip, watching the pulsating patterns that fluctuated across the surface.

Finally, the *baru* rose and joined his associates who were solemnly discussing the patterns of spilt hen's blood, and which astronomical signs bordering the circle had been indicated by being thus spattered. Their bald heads bobbed this way and that as they debated amongst themselves.

A short distance away stood the king and his generals, silently watching and waiting for the *baru* and the *mashmashus* to make their pronouncements.

Ninus' chief-of-arms, a steel-eyed soldier, leaned close to the king and whispered hoarsely, "A dying *chicken* determines our war strategy, my Lord?"

Shifting his eyes toward the grimacing warrior, the king coolly replied, "Lugal-zagesi, old friend, we need the priests and diviners if we are to control the masses of people. Besides," the king said almost to himself, "have you not experienced the power they represent? I have!"

Lugal-zagesi knew when to hold his tongue.

Finally, the tense whisperings of the priests and diviners came to an end. The *baru* stepped toward the king, his face smeared with chicken blood, and announced imperiously, "Attack the day after tomorrow O' king, just before dawn! The gods will deliver your enemies into your hand!"

That was all the king and his generals needed to hear.

⇥ ⇤

Back in Babylon, two young women made their way down Amurru Street toward the canal that ran through their neighborhood. One of them, Miriam, balanced her empty water jar on her head, while her friend Vashti, the daughter of Enna-nedu, carried hers in her arms while she cried inconsolably.

Arriving at the place where women and girls came to get water for household use, the friends sat down, knowing they needed more time to talk before they went back to their own homes. A distraught Vashti spoke first.

"I thought I knew him, Miriam. I thought he was a believer in

El Shaddai, like we and our families are," she wailed. "His mother and father are godly people too. They don't believe in these new gods any more than we do. How can this happen, Miriam? How can Reza turn away from our God and accept these imposters? Doesn't he know that El Shaddai sent the Flood to destroy the people for rejecting him and turning to these other beings?"

Miriam held her friends' hand and softly cried with her. Vashti used the hem of her head covering to dab at her eyes. Looking into her friend's face, she continued to struggle through her inner turmoil.

"Miriam," she said sternly, "can I have a pagan for a husband? Could I have idols in my home? Could I raise children that way?"

Vashti pulled her knees up and wrapped her arms around them and began to rock back and forth sobbing. "I love him, Miriam! What should I do? What would you do?"

Miriam looked at her suffering friend and said "You have to do what your heart tells you Vashti, but you must be faithful to God above all. My father says that God always has a faithful remnant, those who stay true to him and don't worship things that are not God. We are that remnant, Vashti. Stay faithful to God — El Shaddai — and he will care for you, in this life and in the next."

After a few more minutes the girls rose and filled their water jars, and balancing them on their heads, began the walk back to their homes. When the time came to part company, Miriam turned to her friend and said "What will you do, Vashti?"

"I will pray," she replied.

CHAPTER THIRTEEN

The Destruction of Dur Sharukkin

King Ninus split his forces and had them march through the desert in wide arcs, one flank to the east and one to the west of Dur Sharukkin. Thus, the town would come under attack from two directions simultaneously and would not be able to present a unified defense.

Under cover of darkness, the king's foot soldiers quietly trod, single-file, into the hills and ravines surrounding Dur Sharukkin. No flame or beacon was allowed, no word spoken. Several hundred yards behind the infantry, the mounted lancers and charioteers quieted their steeds.

The worried bleating of the town's flocks of sheep and the concerned lowing of the cattle caused no undue alarm to those few individuals who stirred at that early morning hour, for jackals and wild dogs were not uncommon.

All was tense, and still. Deathly still.

Then a great blast from a horn shattered the pre-dawn darkness as hundreds of infantrymen poured into Dur Sharukkin from both ends of the town's main east-west roadway. Divide and conquer. Fanning out into the streets and alleyways, the soldiers began kicking their way into homes and putting each person found to the sword. Screaming women with babies in their arms fled from their homes only to be cut down in the street, and then watch horrified and dying as their little ones were mercilessly stabbed, trampled, or dashed against walls.

The townsmen tried to gather into small pockets of resistance, but armed only with farming implements they were quickly cut down. Fires sprouted all over Dur Sharukkin as everything that would burn was torched.

As dawn began to creep over the horizon and darkness gave way to first light, hundreds of survivors fled, panic-stricken and clutching children, into the fields surrounding Dur Sharukkin.

A double blast from the horn set the Babylonian archers in action. Ringing the fields around Dur Sharukkin, the archers released deadly volleys of arrows into the fleeing townspeople, who now realized, with shock and added grief, that they had run from one deadly trap into another. Caught between the archers and their burning town, now overrun with murderous foot soldiers, the survivors paused, at a loss as what to do next.

At a triple blast of the horn, the king's chariots rumbled into the fray, the drivers weaving and turning among the running Sharukkans at will. Each chariot wheel had sharp, whirling blades protruding from the hub that severed or mangled the legs of fleeing victims. The charioteers, drove their deadly vehicles mercilessly over those who had fallen.

Finally, perhaps needlessly, the horn was given a quadruple blast, sending the mounted lancers charging into the remaining survivors, running each one down like a hunted animal, impaling him or her to the ground.

The sun rose on a grisly scene of death and smoldering destruction. Ninus had provided his soldiers with a monetary incentive and the time had come to tally the results. Shocking even his own generals, the king had declared that he would pay the soldiers a bounty for each person they killed, the evidence of which would be the victim's *head*.

Piles of severed heads were being heaped up all through the town and its surrounding fields, each grisly pile watched over by an exhausted, bloodstained soldier who jealously guarded his trophies. The king's accountants were making their way from one stack of heads to another, noting the name of the soldier and the number of heads he had collected.

"One *shiklu* per head!" the king had announced at the muster just prior to the army's departure for Dur Sharukkin. One *shiklu* meant one days' pay to a soldier. An effective incentive it was, for other than a prescribed number of adult male prisoners, there were no survivors left in Dur Sharukkin, and no corpse with a head attached to it.

Ninus stood on a hilltop surveying the destruction. His chief accountant, having just received a preliminary 'head count', glanced at the king and shook his head with a weary sigh.

"It's worth the price!" said the king, reading his accountant's mind. "Keep in mind the value of the goods we'll retrieve here. And the bitumen pits! No more exorbitant fees for the products we need for our temples and public works! Yes, it's well worth the price! This is to be our standard war strategy from this day forward!" Then, with a nod to the accountant, he added "Maybe we'll pay a little less per head from now on."

The chief accountant returned the nod and smiled weakly, but when Ninus turned away, he stared into the distance, filled with dread.

"This is insanity!" the accountant thought to himself. "We have become nothing more than brute beasts!"

Another devilish thought had occurred to Ninus as he made his plans for the destruction of Dur Sharukkin. Not only would every man, woman, and child there pay with their lives. Not only would all of their valuables and livestock be confiscated. That was, somehow, not enough. "No one will ever live there again!" he decided.

The planners were puzzled over the king's order to stock enormous, unnecessary quantities of salt. "Why salt?" they queried amongst themselves. "Wagonload after wagonload of *salt!*"

Now that the destruction of Dur Sharukkin was accomplished, they would find out what the king had in mind.

For now, on the command of Ninus, the soldiers were pulling down what remained of buildings and other structures in the devastated village. The rubble was hauled to the smoldering dump outside of town and disposed. As a final act of aggression, the wagonloads of salt were brought in, dumped around the site of the village, then spread over the entire area and plowed under with ox-drawn plows. This being done, the area would be forever desolate.

Ninus surveyed his handiwork with great satisfaction from the hilltop. His generals, who stood with him, eyed him warily. The king *did* have a regal bearing. He stood taller than average, his long black hair and beard curled in flowing ringlets. His face was sharply chiseled with a rather large hooked nose, full lips, dark complexion, and black piercing eyes that bore straight through a person. He was now clad in a scarlet robe lined with gold embroidery and a gold sash. His sandals were laced up almost to his knees. He carried a saber at his side, and an ivory-handled dagger in his sash. He had a nervous habit of touching and caressing the handle of the dagger with the tips of his fingers, a habit that made those in his presence nervous as well.

Impressed, or awed, as they were, the generals could sense that they were caught up in something monstrous, something much bigger and far-reaching than they could imagine. Something had been unleashed on humanity that could not be stopped now.

Ninus spun around and faced his generals. "Nebu-sarsekim, have the bodies been burned?" The general replied, "It is being done as we speak, my Lord. We have also kept alive sixty Sharukka men, per your instructions."

The king turned to the next man. "Nergal-shahrezer, what is the disposition of the towns' wealth?"

The fat, squatty general, absentmindedly curling his beard, said, "All salvageable items of value were retrieved prior to the, er... ah, salting of the area, my Lord. Everything has been cataloged by the scribes and stored on wagons."

Ninus leaned forward, his face just inches from Nergal-shahrezer's and said through clenched teeth, "And who, pray tell, is guarding the wagons?"

"Uh, four guards to a wagon Lord Ninus!" Nergal-shahrezer hastily replied, "All good men, my Lord!"

Ninus gave the fat general a sidelong glance. "Assign men to guard the guards. The punishment for theft will be severe, for the thief *and* his family! If anyone steals, he steals from the gods!" said Ninus. "And I am the right arm of the gods! Inform the men."

Struck suddenly with what he deemed a good idea, the king turned and summoned his personal assistant, who quickly appeared and bowed clasping his hands before his face.

"Arioch," Ninus smiled, pleased with himself, "have messengers deliver the head of one of our Sharukka friends to every town and village in the area. The head is to be set on a pike in the public square of the village. The messengers shall summon the villagers and tell them "This is the fate of all who resist Nimrod!"

Arioch blanched and started to ask the king if he meant what he had just said. Then, realizing that the king *had* meant what he said, he backed away and stood up straight, and gasping for breath, said, "At once Lord Ninus!"

"Oh, Arioch," Ninus said, his face brightening with another idea. "The name of this town — Sharukkin, 'Righteous Ruler' — I like it! Write that down, Arioch! That shall be one of my titles — Sharukkin, the Righteous Ruler!"

"Well chosen Lord Ninus." said the aide dutifully.

Now buoyant, the king turned to his generals, and giving each one a congratulatory slap on the back, said merrily, "Make sure the men are well provided with food and drink tonight. Send some men into the villages in the area to round up some local women for the soldiers to enjoy. Tonight we all eat meat and drink wine! We leave tomorrow... mid-morning."

Above the bloody battleground, unseen by human eyes, multitudes of spirits also rejoiced and congratulated one another. A pattern had just been established. Organized deliberate violence and destruction on a grand scale was now possible, indeed inevitable, inflicted by man upon man in the name of pride and greed. Violence against innocent civilians had now been established as an instrument of government policy. Now there was no limit to human suffering.

The great cosmic mystery — free will permitted by God to have its way contrary to his will — began to operate in the realm of human governance.

Holy angels of heaven looked on in bewilderment.

"The Creator permits his enemies to do *this?*" some said wonderingly.

But angels of the higher orders reproved them: "Do not forget the mystery of the Holy One, El Shaddai, that through his people on Earth he will make his boundless manifold wisdom known to the rulers and authorities in the heavenly realms. Watch!" the higher angels admonished. "Observe carefully! Do not let the lessons be lost as God's people suffer the things they must suffer at the hands of our enemies, and theirs!"

The next morning the king's chief-of-arms, with the old-fashioned Sumerian name, Lugal-zagesi, stood watching, his arms folded across his chest. A long winding caravan of Babylonian soldiers with animals, prisoners, and wagons laden with loot, passed before him heading south. The Babylonian army left behind a large flat salt-encrusted area that, until recently, had been a bustling town of some 3000 souls.

In the middle of the entourage were sixty prisoners, all adult men, trudging dejectedly in pairs, each man's arms lashed together behind his back at the elbows and wrists. Ninus wanted trophies to bring back home, and the number sixty had tremendous occultic significance to the priests and mathematicians.

The king, mounted on a black stallion, rode at the head of his troops. His aide, Arioch, rode beside him deep in thought. Before them lay some one hundred and eighty miles of mostly desolate country, but by following the course of the Tigris River southward

Ninus knew his troops and animals would be well watered.

As the army meandered southward the king rode up to the crest of a rocky hill, and looking around, espied a wide flat area to his left. Summoning Arioch and his generals to join him, Ninus pointed out to them the green and fertile area, with its lush date palms, and made an impromptu decision.

"We have destroyed a city," he announced, and with a sweeping gesture of his arm, pointed to the fertile site now before them and proclaimed, "and we shall build a new one, there!"

"Nebu-zaradan" the king said, turning to his general, "you will remain behind with a crew of surveyors and lay out a city plan similar to the ones under construction in Erek, Akkad, and Kalneh. When we arrive in Babylon I will send architects, engineers, and laborers."

Nebu-zaradan, still trying to take in the scope of his new assignment, struggled to speak. "But, but, Lord Ninus, a new city?" He paused, searching for words. "Who will populate it? What will we call it?"

The king now turned his gaze forcefully on Nebu-zaradan and replied "*Find people,* General! Were you just born yesterday? What did we do in Erek, Akkad, and Kalneh? Dismantle other villages, relocate the people. We have other conquests before us. We will send people here. Oh, and 'what will we call it'?" Ninus sat erect in his saddle and paused dramatically. "I will name it after myself! The city will be named *Nineveh*, the City of Ninus!"

Without another word he reined his horse around and resumed his way toward Babylon. The bewildered generals looked at each other and shook their heads.

The army camped the next night 20 miles further south. The

following morning the caravan of men and animals made ready to depart. Summoning General Nergal-shahrezer, the king issued another unexpected command.

"I wish another city to be built, on this site," he said casually. Nergal-shahrezer's countenance fell. He *so* wanted to return to his home and wife and children. He waited for the hammer to fall.

"*You* will build it General! It will also bear my name — my *new* name. It will be called 'Nimrod'! Engineers and laborers will arrive within a month."

The chief priest, the *sa anga,* stood nearby waiting for the king to finish giving the general his instructions. As Ninus turned to walk away he ran into the *sa anga* who stumbled backwards and almost fell. Recovering himself, the *sa anga* apologized profusely, then reminded the king, "My Lord, please remember the time! The month Nisan approaches. We must return to Babylon in time for the start of the New Year Festival!"

The king tapped his own forehead in a mock gesture of forgetfulness.

"Of course! What *was* I thinking? The Newwww Year Festival! What is it I'm supposed to do, you know, at the climax of the festival, *sa-anga?*"

The high priest replied solemnly "The king must submit to Marduk!"

Hovering unseen, in and around the king, the spirit Marduk chuckled menacingly, "Oh yes, *that* you will!"

CHAPTER FOURTEEN

Lovers Confrontation

Back in Babylon, the mood was tense in the home of Zakir, the brick-maker. He and his son Reza were hardly on speaking terms after their disruptive scene outside the home of Vashti. There had been much discussion, most of it combative and upsetting, but for now the combatants had withdrawn from each other and an icy aloofness pervaded the once festive home.

From Zakir's point of view, Reza was abandoning the true faith in the only God, the invisible Creator — El Shaddai. Reza, on the other hand, saw himself as a seeker. He had become convinced that there were other paths to ultimate truth. Faith in God did not produce anything tangible for him; or if there *was* anything tangible, it came much too slow for Reza's liking.

'There must be a shortcut to spiritual knowledge,' he thought. 'The walk of faith is too slow.'

Reza's mother, Ishabi, was distraught and exhausted. She could not sleep at night for worry over her wayward son.

Reza's personal agony concerned his love, Vashti. He had not seen her or talked to her since he had revealed his intention to join the priesthood of Marduk. He ached to see her, to say kind things to her, to hold her hand and know that things were alright between them.

One morning, when he could bear it no longer, he called a foreman from the brickyard and told him "I'm leaving early for the mid-day meal. Tell my father when you see him."

The foreman bowed, raising his clasped hands to his forehead, and replied, "I will, Master Reza."

Reza started out walking from his father's business, but as he got closer to Zababa Street, where the market was, his speed increased. Then, as he turned on Zababa Street and saw all the market activity, he could not help breaking out into a run, constantly swerving, barely avoiding collisions, and leaping over piles and bundles of merchandise.

When he finally spotted Vashti's fabric stall he slowed down to catch his breath and compose himself. Fumbling in the pocket of his tunic, Reza found a mint leaf to chew on, in case his breath was stale.

Just as his heart calmed, he saw Vashti up ahead, spreading fabric samples in front of her mother's stall, and his heart began to race again.

'My beliefs don't change how I feel about Vashti,' the young man murmured to himself. 'It's our love that matters!'

Feeling buoyed now, Reza shouted out to his love, "Hello, Vashti!"

However, his heart sank when Vashti looked up startled, and seeing Reza, whirled around and fled into her mother's stall.

Stunned at first, Reza stuck out his jaw, undeterred, and marched up to the fabric stall. For the sake of propriety he addressed Vashti's mother first.

"Greetings Enna-nedu. May I please speak with Vashti?"

When the woman turned to face him her look was fierce and

she minced no words.

"How dare you abandon your God, young man? El Shaddai created you to give him glory, but now you shame him by turning to worthless idols of false gods. Not only that, but you shame your parents who love you and taught you the truth about El Shaddai. You have broken their hearts! And if that is not enough, my daughter, she,... her heart has been,... I will say no more!"

Enna-nedu turned to confer with her daughter, who stood with her back to Reza. The two robed figures conversed silently for a moment, then Vashti turned and looked up at Reza in an emotional turmoil of love, anger, and confusion. Stepping out of her stall, Vashti approached Reza and said sharply "We will buy something from the fruit seller's stall," and motioned for him to come with her.

Reza had never seen Vashti walk so fast. He spoke quickly as he struggled to keep up with her.

"Vashti, my decision doesn't have to ruin everything. I'm still me!"

She looked straight ahead and said nothing.

"Our future is what matters!" Reza shouted. "I love you Vashti! Doesn't that mean anything to you?"

They were now standing beside a large circular fountain in the middle of the busy marketplace. Vashti motioned for Reza to sit down on the brick border surrounding the fountain, then she sat down beside him. She pulled back her head covering, exposing her long dark hair, and looked directly into Reza's face with tear-filled eyes. Reza braced himself.

"Yes, Reza," Vashti began slowly, "our love does mean something to me. I have dreamed of being your wife since I was a little girl. I used to watch you playing with the other boys in the street. You were always the leader. People looked up to you even then. So did I. Marrying you and bearing your children is the dream of my life! But now you're making a deadly mistake! Would I be loving you if I accepted the fact that you were rejecting the only true God for false gods who are nothing but rebellious spirits? Would I be loving you if I encouraged you to put your very soul in danger? Would I be loving you if I encouraged you to go down a path to your own destruction?"

Vashti became defiant. "What about our children, Reza?" "Would I be loving our children if I allowed idols to be set up in our home? Would I be a loving mother if I stood by and let my children be led into false worship? It is the worship of demons, Reza!" she hissed, with tears streaming down her face.

Vashti looked around as if pleading for help.

"The king's priests are sick and corrupt," she continued. "They will corrupt you too! They will encourage you to lie with the temple prostitutes and take the drugs and potions that make them crazy. You will become lost and separated from our God, El Shaddai. You will become a curse to me and to our children."

Vashti sat up straight and faced Reza calmly. "No, Reza," she said with finality, "I would not be loving you if I agreed to your own destruction. Will you turn away from this madness and ask God to forgive you?"

It was Reza's turn to become defiant.

He grabbed Vashti by the wrist. "What gives you the right to be so righteous?" he said angrily.

She jerked her hand away, glaring at him.

He continued, "Why do you and our parents think you have all the answers to everything? Maybe you just don't! There is more to the priests than you know about. They know the secrets of the universe! They will teach me about the stars and planets, about numbers, and every kind of plant. They will even teach me how to write! Just think of it, Vashti — me! They already told me about the 'ascended masters', the lords — the *baalim* — who rule in the spirit world. I haven't seen them yet, but I'm told they are wise and kind."

"The priests want to initiate me. They think I am worthy!" Reza said, unable to control his excitement.

Vashti stood and looked down at him. "El Shaddai is the only true God, and I am his child," she said in a whisper. "If you reject him, you reject me. There would never really be peace between us, Reza, and we would lose God's blessings."

Vashti pulled her head covering over her head and turned and walked away.

Reza cried out, "Vashti, wait!"

Getting no response, he hung his head dejectedly and muttered to himself, "Now what?"

CHAPTER FIFTEEN

The New Year Festival Begins

Shivering in the pre-dawn chill, the high priest, the *sa anga*, impatiently eyed the eastern horizon from atop the temple of the sun god Shamash in Babylon. This was the moment that he and the other astrologers had carefully calculated and predicted months ago.

Finally, a tiny sliver of light appeared in the east. The *sa anga* stepped back and repositioned himself to visually align the rising sun with a strategically placed bronze marker on a stone altar. The marker indicated where the sun would appear at sunrise on the morning of the spring equinox.

Satisfied now, the *sa anga* stood to his full height, and raising his hands skyward, majestically declared, "Shamash arises at his appointed place!"

Upon that pronouncement subordinate priests and functionaries wordlessly scattered to their appointed tasks like cockroaches in the dark. The spring equinox had officially arrived, marking the first day of the month Nisan, and hence the start of the Babylonian new year.

As darkness yielded to first light, it could be seen that the city of Babylon was festooned with colorful, fluttering banners representing the gods Anu, Enlil, Ea, Ishtar, Adad, Shamash, and the moon god Sin. Red banners were especially conspicuous, for these were the banners of the *mu-shushu* — the 'raging dragon' — of the god Marduk, and rumor had it that this was to be *his* celebration.

The great city itself was undergoing a transformation as ambitious public works projects progressed. These included the construction of massive city walls, moats, avenues, temples, palaces, soldiers' barracks, administrative buildings, and canal systems that looped right through the city and flowed back into the Euphrates River. A bridge had just been completed over the river and plans were already being carried out to expand the city on both sides.

At the north end of town, construction was underway on a magnificent entryway through the city wall, to be called the Ishtar Gate. The gateway honored the people's beloved Queen of Heaven, the goddess of sexual love, and of war and bloodshed. She was the great celestial mother, but she was also capable of rage and violence. She was known to be wildly promiscuous, taking many lovers both of gods and humans.

Even with such great public works underway the king and his ministers had an even more important focus. The temple of Shamash, called *Esagila*, the 'Abode of the Great God', stood in an area known locally as the Sacred Precinct. This area on the east bank of the Euphrates River was now being expanded to include the construction of a massive seven-tiered pyramid, known as a *ziggurat*, to be dedicated to a deity as yet unannounced.

A wall of blue enameled brick was being built to surround the entire Sacred Precinct, while a new roadway ran straight through the site, separating the Temple of Shamash from the new *ziggurat*. The road continued westward through the city gate and over the bridge to the new town development on the other side of the Euphrates.

Finally, a great monumental boulevard had been constructed leading from the east entrance of the Sacred Precinct northward through the city to the Ishtar Gate. This raised roadway was named the Processional Way. Ninus had been particularly anxious to have this roadway finished by the start of the New Year Festival. The road sloped gently upwards as it approached the Ishtar Gate and was lined on either side by walls twenty feet tall, made of bright blue enameled brick. The brilliantly colored walls featured bas-relief bulls, representing the god Adad, and carved *mu-shushu* dragons of Marduk, spaced every twenty yards.

The Processional Way was about to be put to its designed use, for by mid-morning on New Year's day, the roadway was already lined along its sides and the top of its walls, with excited, jostling Babylonians of every age and status. Even slaves, the *wardum*, could take part in the New Year's festivities.

The excitement continued to mount as people streamed toward the Processional Way and the Sacred Precinct from all parts of town, then rose to a fever pitch as heralds at the Ishtar Gate began to blow their trumpets.

The spectators gasped and strained to look as the doors of the Ishtar Gate slowly opened and trumpeters began marching through playing their instruments. Then came a squadron of drummers methodically pounding their marching beats on skin-covered drums.

Close behind the drummers danced dozens of the prettiest girls in the land, barefoot, wearing white linen dresses, their long hair flowing in the morning breeze as they gracefully whirled and leaped along the Processional Way.

Then, to everyone's delight, a herd of little boys, dressed in mock soldier uniforms, with mock swords, came stampeding through the Ishtar Gate. The laughter of the crowds followed them down the boulevard as the lads engaged one another in duels or tried to appear serious and march 'like the big soldiers'.

Next, the priests of the gods of Babylon, along with their attendants and trainees, paraded solemnly, swinging smoking incense burners and mumbling dark and incomprehensible utterances.

The priests had designed for themselves the oddest headgear, called mitres. These were tall cone shaped hats, that when seen from above, resembled a fish head with its mouth open. Flowing from the back of the priest's mitre down to his ankles were two strips of cloth that were intended to give the appearance of a fish's spine and fins. According to the temple attendants this bizarre headgear was designed to honor Ea, the god of the oceans. Ea would be known to other nations as Dagon, Oannes, Neptune, and Poseidon.

The crowds' attention then turned to the king's troops who were now filing through the already impressive, but unfinished gateway. The banner bearers led the way, holding aloft the red *mushushu* dragon emblems of Marduk, which had now been adopted as the king's war insignia. Then the generals entered through the archway followed by their foot-soldiers. The soldiers held their shields and spears in front of them in a defensive mode. Each man pounded his spear against his shield after every third pace, producing a thunderous effect, to the people's delight.

Following the infantry came the archers, each man equipped with bow and quiver. Every twenty paces, in unison, the archers reached back over their shoulders and grabbed an arrow from their quivers, then placing it in their bows, they pulled the bowstrings back, aiming at the sky, as if to release a deadly volley.

Next in the procession were the mounted lancers, capes rustling in the breeze, each one on a decorated prancing steed. The girls in the crowd flirted with the lancers by tossing flower garlands over the tips of their upthrust lances. The soldiers played along by tipping their lances even higher to allow the garlands to slide down to their grasp. The girls swooned and giggled as the men then placed the flowers around their own necks and sent a smile to the girl who threw it.

Following the lancers came the war chariots, easily the crowd favorite thus far. The proud charioteers saluted the crowds as their squires steered the vehicles, which now had their vicious whirling blades removed for the safety of the crowd.

After the charioteers had passed on down the Processional Way toward the Sacred Precinct there was a pause in the parade and the crowd started to become impatient, wondering what was next. The pause was carefully orchestrated, for what followed brought a deafening roar of approval from the people.

The clattering outside the gate came to a stop, paused, then dramatically began again as King Nimrod, the Rebel rode in before the cheering masses in a gleaming bronze chariot, driven by an officer. The king appeared to the people as a god dressed in a red robe, lavishly decorated with the signs and insignia of the false gods that he and his queen, Semiramis, had led the people to worship in the place of their true Creator and Heavenly Father.

In his right hand he carried a sword, as the symbol of his earthly power and authority. In his left hand he carried a measuring cord indicating his divine authority in determining the lives and destinies of humans. On his head he wore a conical, ribbed headdress that would be known to later generations in that land as that of a priest-king, one who ruled the people not just in an earthly sense but also with regard to spiritual matters. He ruled on earth as the representative of the gods, the connection and mediator between men and gods. He received wisdom from heaven and the divine right to rule.

The smile on Nimrod's face belied his true thoughts as he basked in the adulation of the cheering, waving crowd. For as he gazed at them he thought, 'I am your god you worthless eaters! You exist to serve me and the great god Lucifer, the Bringer of Light! Your only purpose is to worship us and give us your life force!'

The masses cheered. Women threw flowers. The King smiled and waved.

Bringing up the end of the victory procession, trudging silently, were the sixty male captives from Dur Sharukkin. The men were still bound tightly with their arms behind their backs but in order to further humiliate them, long saplings had been cut and were intertwined about their necks, like yoked oxen. They could do nothing but shuffle forward in a straight line as their guards poked and prodded them with swords and spears.

Although of a different tribe than the Babylonians, these men were their brothers, speaking a similar dialect and having the same ancestry and heritage. They had committed no wrong against the Babylonians. They now received no mercy.

First the young boys, then the adult spectators, began throwing rocks and shouting curses and insults at the grieving, starved prisoners. As the last of the prisoners passed through the Ishtar Gate and started down the Processional Way toward the Sacred Precinct — and their certain doom — the now riotous crowd fell in behind them and made itself the end of the parade.

Later that afternoon, in the courtyard of the Sacred Precinct, the Sharukka prisoners were ceremonially executed by decapitation. Their last act was to pray for God's forgiveness and mercy for the Babylonians. This pious regard for their brothers and sisters was met with insults, derision, and an ax.

So the people gave their full consent and cooperation to the joining of evil forces, human and spirit, that were now combined to instigate human misery on the Earth.

As above, so below.

CHAPTER SIXTEEN

As Above, So Below

"*Ludlul Bel Nemeki!* I will praise the lord of wisdom!" shouted the high priest from the top step of the Temple of the Sun God. With arms still upraised he looked down upon a vast crowd filling the entire Sacred Precinct of Esagila. The mob, which included not only the residents of Babylon but also people from all the surrounding villages and countryside, shouted in response, '*Ludlul Bel Nemeki!*'

At that signal the baldheaded temple attendants began pouring sacks of powdery incense onto hot coals burning on brazen altars erected at either side of the high priest. Thus began the festivities on day two of the Babylonian New Year Festival.

Swooning in a drug-induced frenzy with clouds of incense rising around him, the high priest, the *sa anga,* stretched out his bare left arm, and reaching over with a knife in his right hand, slit the inside of his forearm. Quickly switching the knife to his left hand, he made a gash in his right arm. All the other priests with him raised knives and inflicted similar wounds on their own bodies. Then, lifting both hands skyward to let the blood run down his arms, the *sa anga* began a loud invocation to the gods:

> "Spirits of the celestial bodies, we praise you!
> O' mighty gods of the constellations, hear us!
> O' great astral spirits receive our praise!

O' great Anu, remember us!
O' great Enlil, remember us!
O' great Ea, remember us!
O' great Shamash, remember us!
O' great Marduk, remember us!
O' great Adad, remember us!
O' great Ishtar, remember us!
O' great Ninurta, remember us!
O' great Kishar, remember us!
O' great Nergal, remember us!
O' great Sin, remember us!
O' great Nebu, remember us!

O' gods of all the earth and heavens
we call on you!
Your servants beseech you!
May you smile on us and bless us!
May you richly bless the king and grant him health and eternal
    life!
Bless the bounty of our fields and our animals!
Bless the womb and the hearth!

We praise the great celestial gods!
May they be eternally blessed!"

"May they be eternally blessed!" roared the crowd.

Having invoked their gods the people resumed drinking and merrymaking in the streets of Babylon. The priests however, quickly retired to an inner chamber in the temple of Shamash where they ingested more of the mind-altering potions they had taken earlier to ease the pains of their self-inflicted wounds.

In the whirling vortex over the festive city Chulgomet addressed the spirits.

"I must confess I am almost giddy with excitement Colleagues! Things are going so well I can hardly take it all in! You yourselves saw our devoted priests abusing their own bodies! Here is a principle you all must remember for it comes directly from Lord Lucifer: self-abuse performed in pursuit of self-directed spirituality is especially offensive to the Creator who made the humans in his own image. These self-inflicted mortifications do nothing but draw their attention to their own worthless selves. And we crave the shedding of their blood. This being the case, we must do whatever we can to encourage it."

Chulgomet glanced around as a murmur of approval went up from the massive swarm of spirits swirling and pulsating all around him. Pausing dramatically, he continued. "Under the direction of our Lord Lucifer we have succeeded in instigating among the humans the worship of the stars, constellations, and planetary bodies. Through our suggestions and visitations the priests have developed a *zodiac*, or 'circle of animals', through which they believe they can predict future events, as well as ascertain human characteristics and behavior.

"We *foresee*," Chulgomet added humorously, "that this simple device will endlessly distract many, many people away from productive activities and will lead them into a fruitless and pointless effort to know what lies ahead of them in life. We have injected just enough of our wisdom into this system to attract them and give them a sense of power, as well as the deliciously prideful feeling of having secret knowledge.

"We have also instilled the wretches with an obsession to

observe the skies, measuring the movements of the planets and stars relative to Earth. They are already planning their lives and activities around the solstices and equinoxes. Why, they even kill animals and other humans as blood sacrifices to mark these ordinary celestial events! We have them imagining that all sorts of things come to pass depending on the size and shape of Earth's shadow on the moon! Astounding!

"I have received a report from our colleague Baphomet, who informs us that the humans, through our influence with the priests, are becoming preoccupied with seeking out signs and omens, dreams and portents, visitations and oracles, which lead them away from the Creator to us!

"They are already obsessed with fortune-telling, divination, and communicating with the dead — all forbidden by the Creator — for he knows they are communicating with us.

"We've tricked them into believing that ordinary objects such as stones, crystals, and pieces of wood hold special powers and qualities. They revere these ordinary elements and set them up as idols in their homes, or wear them as amulets and adornments! It is so gratifying to lead them astray!

"Our strategy must be, at all times, to reward their efforts by sharing some of our energy with them, giving them a feeling of power, and of *pride* above all else! This puts them in league with us!"

Chuckling with delight, Chulgomet continued. "Our messengers also inform us of the widespread use of mind and soul stupefying narcotics and potions which not only turn the already idiotic humans into the living dead but also opens them to our influence. We can write whatever we want on a blank mind!

"Some of the meditation techniques we are teaching them tend to accomplish the same thing. Whatever turns them inward and makes them *self*-centered and *self*-focused works to our advantage, for it is then that they become defenseless and unwittingly place themselves outside of God's protection, and under ours. Remember Colleagues, if a human puts up no defense against us we may attack at will! If a man is unarmed and believes he has no enemy, he is doomed!"

A thunderous roar of approval burst from within the vortex.

"One more happy note, Colleagues," continued an ecstatic Chulgomet, "our forces have been extremely successful in promoting the human worship and adoration of idols and images of almost everything! The worthless fools make and adore images of ourselves that we convey to them, as well as images of stars, trees, animals, other humans, literally anything! They seek spiritual truth in symbols, geometric shapes, even numbers! Why, the number seven simply enthralls them! It's baffling! Their gullibility knows no bounds!" he exulted. "'Made in the image of God'...*indeed!*

"The most amazing thing about it all is that our lies and teachings not only lead the human creatures away from God, but also instill in them a false sense of self-righteousness. They are blind and lost but don't know it!

"I do believe, Colleagues," Chulgomet concluded, "that these ignorant jars of clay will worship *anything* but the invisible God who made them. But they do worship us!

"They worship us!" thundered the spirits in the whirling vortex.

Chulgomet nodded, "We are their gods!"

CHAPTER SEVENTEEN

The Enuma Elish

The second and third days of the New Years' Festival consisted of general public debauchery as the people danced, feasted, and drank themselves into a stupor. Normal societal boundaries went largely ignored, including those that bound husbands and wives into monogamous relationships.

The idols of the gods were adorned with gold, silver, and precious jewels, even specially made clothing, and carried through the streets on poles and litters as the people cheered and praised them loudly. The idols were not simply pieces of stone, wood, or metal, for the priests had consecrated them in secret ceremonies. Thus, the idols became identified with actual spirit beings. Rumors were widespread that the statues of the gods were even fed meals in the temple and were entertained by musicians and dancers.

The fourth day of the festival, however, heralded a big event — the reading and enacting of the *Enuma Elish*, the Epic of Creation — the Babylonian version of the creation of the earth and heavens.

A massive stage had been erected for this purpose in the Sacred Precinct between the Temple of Shamash and the mysterious *ziggurat,* or pyramid tower that faced it. The imposing tower rose majestically, and menacingly, over the city. The people of Babylon sensed something dark and foreboding about the tower but no one could lay hold of what it was that really troubled them.

The fourth day passed as had the previous two, with public merry-making and the parading of the precious gods through the streets. However, as the sun began to set, a trumpet blast from the Sacred Precinct drew the people's attention and they began to make their way in its direction eagerly anticipating the night's festivities.

Bronze braziers set up around the perimeter of the stage lit the area with leaping flames. Stationed behind the stage in the darkness were drummers who began beating out a hypnotic rhythm as the crowds filled the Sacred Precinct. Attendants poured incense into the burning braziers producing intoxicating clouds that wafted their way over and among the excited populace.

The crowd stared transfixed as the *sa anga* stepped to the front of the stage, and lifting his hands to the skies, he waited for the people to become silent. When all was still he paused dramatically, then began in a loud voice:

> "Enuma elish la nebu shamamu
> shaplitu amatum shuma la zakrat!"

> "When in the heights heaven had not been
> named, and below, firm ground had not
> been called forth...."

Thus began the Epic of Creation. Unknown to the common folk, the epic had been modified by the Babylonian priests to promote the raising of Marduk to supremacy amongst the gods. Even less known was the fact that this elevation of Marduk was instigated by Ninus and Semiramis. And finally, known only to the king and queen, it was the spirit Marduk himself who visited them and demanded the supreme worship of himself by the Babylonians. These changes would soon become evident.

Having now a spellbound audience, actors and dancers, brilliantly costumed, acted out the roles of the gods, goddesses, demons, and forces of nature. Musical accompaniment and special effects emerged from behind the stage. The *sa anga* continued.

> Nothing existed but primordial Apsu, the Father of the Gods, and Tiamat, the Mother of the Gods. When their waters mingled together no reed hut had been matted, no marsh land had appeared. When no gods whatsoever had been brought into being, uncalled by name, their destinies undetermined — then it was that the gods were formed within Apsu and Tiamat.

The *sa anga* went on to describe the births of the gods, calling them by name — Lahmu, Lahamu, Anshar, Kishar, Anu, Ea — and many, many others.

As time went on, these divine offspring created such an on-going disturbance that Apsu could get no rest.

> The divine offspring of Apsu and Tiamat banded together, they disturbed Tiamat as they surged back and forth. Yes, they troubled the mood of Tiamat by their hilarity in the Abode of Heaven. Apsu could not lessen their clamor and Tiamat was speechless at their ways. Their doings were loathsome.

Not knowing what else to do, Apsu called his advisor, Mummu, and approached Tiamat, announcing his plans to destroy their children. Tiamat became enraged and grieved at this and urged less severe discipline.

She cried 'What? Should we destroy what we have created?
Their ways are troublesome, but let us tend to them kindly!'

But the scheming Mummu gave advice more to the Primordial Father's liking:

Do destroy their mutinous ways O Father, for then you shall have relief by day and rest by night!' When Apsu heard this his face grew radiant and he considered the evil he had planned against the gods, his children. As for Mummu, Apsu embraced him and kissed him.

Word of this reached the other gods who were at first stunned, then assembled to discuss their strategy. Ea, the all-wise, took matters into his own hands, and having bound Apsu, slew him. Ea then retired to the depths of the oceans with his wife, Damkina, where he established his cult and produced a child named Marduk.

In the chamber of fates, the abode of destinies, a god was engendered, most potent and wisest of gods. In the heart of the depths Marduk was created. He who begot him was Ea, his father; she who conceived him was Damkina, his mother.

From a raised viewing platform in the audience, the king and queen now leaned forward in their seats, their hearts pounding. Their ambition was nothing less than the control and subjugation of the human race, and now with their eyes riveted on the high priest, they watched as an important piece of their strategy unfolded.

Alluring was the figure of Marduk, sparkling were his eyes, lordly was his stride, commanding as a great one of olden times. When

Ea saw him, the father who begot him, he exulted and glowed, his heart was filled with gladness. He had created him perfect and endowed him with a double godhead. Greatly exalted was he above the gods, perfect beyond comprehension! He had four eyes and four ears; when he moved his lips, fire blazed forth. Clothed with the halo of ten gods, he was strong to the utmost.

The king and queen knew, and the priests knew, that in the original text of the Creation Epic, the *Enuma Elish*, it was the god *Enlil* who was exalted to supremacy among the gods, not Marduk.

Meanwhile, the audience, bound to three dimensional vision, could not see the spiritual battle raging in the air over the stage. Warring angels of God were joined in combat with spiritual forces of evil, enemies of both God and man.

As the melee roiled unseen above his head, the *sa anga* continued his monologue while costumed figures whirled and danced around him acting out the parts.

To confront Ea and the other gods who conspired to kill Apsu, Tiamat elevated another god, Kingu, and made him the commander-in-chief of her forces, which included a horrible brood of demon-monsters she gave birth to just for that purpose.

She elevated Kingu and made him chief among them, the leader of the ranks, commander of the assembly. She entrusted these things to him as she seated him in the council. 'I have cast for you the spell, exalting you in the assembly of the gods!' she declared.

Ea was despondent, seeing no way to defeat Tiamat and Kingu. However, his father Anshar proposed to conscript Ea's son Marduk to lead the attack.

> Lord Anshar, father of gods, rose up in grandeur, and having
> pondered the matter in his heart, he said to the assembly of the
> *Annunaki*, the rank and file gods,

> 'He whose strength is potent shall be our avenger — he who is
> mighty in battle — Marduk, the hero!'

Marduk agreed, but with a stipulation: he was to be elevated to
supremacy among the gods!

> If I, Marduk, am indeed to be your avenger and to vanquish
> Tiamat and save your lives, then summon the *Annunaki* to the
> assembly hall, the *Ubshukina*, and proclaim my destiny supreme!
> Let my word determine the fates. What I bring into being shall
> be unalterable; neither shall the command of my lips be recalled
> nor changed!

The *Annunaki* greeted one another in the great assembly hall
and proceeded to feast and drink themselves into a stupor.

> They ate festive bread and partook of the wine. They filled their
> drinking vessels with sweet intoxicants. As they drank the strong
> drink they became bloated and lethargic and their spirits rose.
> 'You are the most honored of the great gods' they declared, 'Your
> decrees are unrivalled, your command is the command of heaven!
> We have granted you kingship over the entire universe! When you
> sit in the assembly your word shall be supreme!'

Having this honor bestowed on him, Marduk proceeded to make
weapons for the slaying of Tiamat. Armed with these, and with seven

evil winds he created, Marduk at last confronted Tiamat:

> How mightily you are arisen; how proudly you exalt yourself! You
> have charged your own heart to stir up conflict so that children
> reject their own fathers. And you hate those that you yourself have
> given birth to!

After charging Tiamat with further crimes against the gods,
he challenged her to single combat. Tiamat, enraged, joined battle
with Marduk, chanting evil spells against him.

> When Tiamat opened her mouth to consume him he drove in the
> evil wind and she could not close her lips against it. As the fierce
> winds charged into her belly, her body became distended and her
> mouth wide open. He released an arrow, it tore her belly, it cut
> through her insides, splitting the heart. Having thus subdued her,
> he extinguished her life.

The crowd in the Sacred Precinct roared its approval as stage
actors, bearing a long dragon-like costume, made the creature twist
and turn, writhing in a death agony.

Tiamat's consort and general, Kingu, was bound and turned
over to Uggae the Lord of Death. Marduk then turned to survey
the fallen mother of the gods.

> Then the Lord Marduk paused to view her dead body, that he
> might divide the monster Tiamat and do artful works. He split her
> like a shellfish into two parts: half of her he set up and established
> as the sky, the other half as Earth.

Having thus created the heavens and the earth, Marduk
prepared to create mankind.

Blood I will mass and cause bones to be. I will create a savage; *man* shall he be called. He will be charged with the service of the gods that they might be at ease!

Marduk then summoned the great Annunaki gods to assembly and he, their king, addressed a word to them. 'Who was it that contrived the uprising and made Tiamat rebel, and joined battle? Let him be handed over who contrived the uprising. His guilt I will make him bear that you may dwell in peace.' Whereupon the Annunaki gods replied to him 'O, *Lugal Dimmerankia,* King of the gods of heaven and earth! It was Kingu who contrived the uprising, and made Tiamat rebel, and joined battle.' They bound Kingu and imposed on him his guilt and severed his blood vessels. Out of his blood they fashioned mankind.

Thus, the Annunaki gods bestowed on Marduk the scepter, the throne, and the royal robe. They declared 'From this day your decrees shall be unrivaled, your command as that of Anu. No one among the gods may transgress your boundaries!'

Having thus completed the epic story of the creation, the *sa anga* then recited fifty divine names and titles for Marduk and described how all the gods bowed down to him to acknowledge his supremacy. Then with arms held high, the *sa anga* ecstatically proclaimed "This is *Bab-ilu* — Babylon — Gateway of the gods!"

Then turning his gaze toward the Temple of Shamash, known as the *Esagila,* 'The Abode of the Great God', he further announced,

"What used to be the temple of Shamash is now the temple of Marduk!"

Nimrod and Semiramis smiled and exchanged knowing glances. Things were moving according to plan.

The *sa anga* now turned his gaze heavenward, and with arms held high began his invocation to Marduk.

> Spirit of the great planet, remember us!
> Marduk, god of victory,
> Marduk, lord of all the lands,
> Marduk, son of Ea, Master of Magicians,
> Marduk, who gives the stars their powers,
> Marduk, who assigns the great Annunaki gods
>   their places, remember us!
> Lord of the worlds and heavenly spaces,
> first among the astral gods, hear us!
> In the name of the covenant sworn between
>   you and the race of men, we call on you!
> Hear us and remember us!
> Marduk, lord of the fifty names, open your gates to us!
> O' great god, lord of the world between the worlds,
> O' great conqueror of the monsters of heaven,
> O' Marduk, hear us and remember us for we
>   are your servants!

The people, as one, echoed back, "We are your servants!"

Above the crowd, in another dimension, Chulgomet glowered at the real Marduk and hissed, "This is an assignment Marduk. Don't let it go to your head!"

Marduk gave Chulgomet a derisive leer and turned away.

CHAPTER EIGHTEEN

The Blood Sacrifice

The rededication of the Temple of Shamash as the Temple of Marduk was as much a political move as it was religious. It was, after all, no small thing to dethrone one deity in favor of another. Albeit a controversial move, the *sa anga* began to see the wisdom of cooperating with the king and queen after watching several of his colleagues being tortured to death, at Semiramis' insistence, for their uncooperative attitudes. However, the *sa anga*, whose name was Shamshi-adad, also realized that powerful institutions were being formed, and he must somehow assert his position now or lose his authority, and those of his successors, permanently.

The rest of the priests, having now received orders from both King and High Priest, began to direct the activities of slaves, servants, craftsmen, and artisans in the task of redesigning and refurbishing the Temple for the use of its new patron god.

The fifth day of the New Year Festival was to hold many surprises.

An angry, muttering Nimrod trudged up the steps of the Esagila, the newly rededicated Temple of Marduk, with his nattering wife, Semiramis, at his side.

"Swallow your pride! For one minute. *One minute*! That's all that's being asked. It will be over in sixty seconds!" the queen hissed at her fuming husband, her eyes blazing.

"One minute, eh?" Nimrod coldly replied "That's how long it would take for me to rip the *sa anga's* guts out and wrap them around his scrawny neck!"

"I don't like him either," she agreed. "but he serves our purposes, and the people are in awe of him."

Stopping at the top of the stairway, the queen turned to her husband, and grabbing him by the arms, stared straight into his face.

"Marduk has spoken to you, has he not, my love?" she murmured.

Her change in tone caught the king by surprise. He first glanced down, then raised his eyes to meet hers. Giving her a knowing look he said "Oh yes, you know I have. I have felt his power surge through me! It was he who gave me the strategies that have brought me such wealth and power over men. A great god he is, worthy of praise!"

Semiramis' eyes narrowed. "Then he is a god worth submitting to!"

Nimrod was trapped. "I'll submit to Marduk, but not to that drug-addled *sa anga!*" he declared bitterly.

"But Marduk has spoken to the *sa anga*, and he demands your submission in the way prescribed!" she snapped back.

The royal couple now had the attention of a crowd of curious onlookers standing in groups around the entrance to the temple at the top of the stairs. These included priests, temple attendants, and the *naditum* — the temple prostitutes — and everyone was wondering what the royal fuss was about.

The queen now stood back regally and delivered her final word on the subject. "Marduk demands your public submission. If you refuse, you lose Marduk, and the power that has brought you everything!"

Realizing there was no way out of his predicament, Nimrod uttered a string of curses and turned to enter the temple.

Upon reaching the top of the Esagila stairway, one passed through a stone arch that led into a rectangular, roofless courtyard. In the center of the courtyard was a fountain in which stood a six foot tall stone phallus. No one knew where the phallic idol had come from, but it was said to be from the pre-flood civilization.

Beyond the fountain was the entrance into the actual temple area of the god. The entrance was decorated with elaborately carved images of the gods and their planets and constellations. Passing through the entrance one entered a dark room, lit with oil lamps on the walls. In the middle of this room was a smoldering incense burner on a stand, beside which was a table with a bronze basin for the ceremonial washing and purification of the priests and ritual objects. At the far end of this room was another doorway, covered by a thick curtain, which led into the holy of holies, the inner sanctum of Marduk.

The eight foot tall statue of Marduk had been hurriedly brought from his shrine in another part of town to its new home in the former Temple of Shamash. The fierce-looking idol, ornately engraved and covered with pure gold, stood on a dais by the far wall of the inner sanctum. Beside it was a gold table, upon which rested the Tablet of Destinies, which described the powers and fates of the gods and the movements of their planets. The walls and ceiling of the room were covered with gold plate.

Shamshi-adad, the *sa anga*, knelt before Marduk, fearfully awaiting the task that had now arrived. If the power and prestige of the priesthood was to be continued, it truly was now or never.

The curtain to the inner sanctum was suddenly brushed aside revealing the angry countenance of the king. Stepping into the holy of holies he paused to allow his eyes to adjust to the gloom, lit only by the flickering lamps set in the walls. The light cast by the flames danced eerily about the room, reflected by the gold-covered walls and ceiling. It seemed to Nimrod that spirits were flitting about the room like bats. His intuition was correct.

The *sa anga* stood stiffly, adjusted his white linen gown, and faced the king. The lamplight made dancing patterns on his bald head. His large round eyes, lined with mascara, bore into the king. His throat constricted as he struggled to swallow.

Drawing himself up, Shamshi-adad tensely addressed the king. "My lord the king must not...he must not enter the holy place of Marduk until his symbols of authority have been removed."

Nimrod gritted his teeth and slowly backed out of the chamber. Stepping out of the inner sanctum the *sa anga* stood face to face with the glowering king, who was joined by an assembly of priests, attendants, and noblemen.

Trembling, the *sa anga* took a deep breath and proceeded with his duty, solemnly announcing:

"The king himself is bound to submission and obedience to the Lord Marduk, as are all mortal men. Your ring of authority please."

The king stiffly extended his right hand while an attendant reached out to remove the ring.

"Touch my ring and you die!" Nimrod growled. "Only the *sa anga* will do this!" The attendant gulped then bowed low and slipped out of sight. The *sa anga* stepped forward and removed the king's ring, then set it on a small cushion held by another attendant. He then reached up and removed the chain from around the king's neck with a medallion bearing the emblem of Marduk, the raging *mu-shushu* dragon. After removing the king's conical crown the *sa anga* handed it to an attendant then turned to face the grimacing king.

To the shock and amazement of all present the *sa anga* reached up with both hands and pulled, hard, on the king's ears. This was an act of punishment and humiliation usually reserved for a disobedient child. Then, before the stunned king could respond, the high priest slapped him across the face!

The terrified *sa anga* took a precautionary step backward and quickly announced in a loud voice,

"The king will now prostrate himself before the Lord Marduk and confess his sins."

To everyone's surprise there was a calm, even placid, expression on the king's face. But the *sa anga* was certain that Nimrod's serene demeanor concealed a murderous rage. The question was not *if* he would exact vengeance but *when* and *how*. But there was a purpose to the high priest's apparent madness, a profound and far-reaching purpose that would reverberate down through the wars and tumult of human history. It was something that Shamsi-adad, the *sa anga*, sensed but was not capable of fully comprehending.

Observing the scene from another dimension, Chulgomet turned to Marduk, Baphomet, and other spirit dignitaries and explained the importance of the moment.

"Focus your energy on the king, Colleagues!" he exclaimed. "This is a critical moment. The king is our arm to inflict violence and chaos on humankind. He also provides us with a material power base, a physical infrastructure that we, as spirit beings, could not otherwise possess. However, if his power is not properly controlled he will eventually ignore us and exalt his own self. This will be true of the leaders we establish and maintain from now on. You have seen Nimrod turn his back on the Creator. Will he not do the same to us if we do not control him?"

Chulgomet continued grimly, "The fleabag humans are capable of shaking their puny fists at God and spirits! The Creator despises this behavior as much as we do! Ironic, is it not? Be that as it may, the power of the king must be balanced by the power of our priesthood, and vice-versa, lest the priests institute their own gods, or themselves as gods! In either case we are abandoned! This must be avoided at all costs! This is a directive from the Lord Lucifer himself!"

Marduk spoke up. "Is it not true, Lord Chulgomet, that the Creator intends to establish his own king who will embody the priestly and kingly functions in one person?"

Chulgomet grimaced. "So say our intelligence sources. But don't forget that *our* Master's method is to counterfeit God's ways so as to confuse and defeat mankind. Our lord's thinking is, 'If God thought of it, then we can use it ourselves, for *our* purposes!' Now, focus your energy on Nimrod!"

The king now stood before the statue of Marduk in the holy of holies. Behind him stood the *sa anga* and several other priests as witnesses. Several noblemen peered from the curtain in the doorway.

Nimrod appeared to swoon, all anger and pride gone from his face. He dropped to his knees on the stone floor as though a mighty unseen hand was forcing him down. Leaning forward, he bowed, touching his forehead to the floor.

The statue of Marduk gazed fiercely on the scene being played out below it, while the spirit called Marduk bore down upon the king, forcing him to his knees. Nimrod began to confess his sins and asked his god Marduk to forgive him and to strengthen him to rule in a worthy manner. After pausing for a moment, the king promised to support the religion and the priesthood, and to maintain the Esagila, the Temple of Marduk.

Shamshi-adad, the high priest of Babylon, grinned with satisfaction.

So did the spirits in the room.

An ashen-faced Nimrod slowly stood, then turned and bowed to the high priest and humbly walked out of the holy of holies.

Shamshi-adad slowly released a great sigh of relief. A bewildered crowd of nobles and temple attendants parted in front of the king to make way. As he was leaving he turned and called for his personal attendant Arioch, who pushed through the crowd and bowed before the king, clasping his hands to his forehead.

All eyes were on Nimrod who spoke softly, "Prepare sackcloth and ashes for me and arrange for a public procession to be conducted immediately; a procession of penitence, led by me."

As Arioch bowed and turned to carry out his orders, the king caught his arm. "Also, my friend," he said, startling everyone, especially Arioch, with his endearing words, "the procession is to be led by a white bull. The procession will end at the steps of the Esagila where the bull will be sacrificed to Marduk."

Nimrod now stared off into space, as though hearing a voice that no one else could hear. With all eyes on him he solemnly declared:

"A blood sacrifice shall be required hereafter, for *without the shedding of blood there will be no forgiveness of sins."*

The *mashmashus* and the royal scribes immediately wrote down Nimrod's new edict, to be carried out in all areas under his dominion.

The vortex over Babylon erupted in a roar of victory as Chulgomet exulted, "Through the corruption of this doctrine we will undo the work of God's future Messiah! We will lead the humans to sacrifice animals, and each other, to *us!* Not only will they receive no forgiveness for their sins, but they will be heaping condemnation on themselves!"

Delirious, Chulgomet screamed: "Thus we smite the Creator!"

CHAPTER NINETEEN

The Initiation Ritual

The streets of Babylon had finally grown quiet and were now illuminated only by a clear moonlit sky. A lone figure ran and stumbled his way through darkened alleys toward one of the city's canals. The exhausted young man paused at the intersection of an alley and a street and gazed up anxiously at the moon above him. He knelt down, panting, and shook dirt from his hair and robe, and wiped blood from his face. Then, hearing footsteps approaching in the dark, he sprang to his feet and ducked down the alley.

He ran, occasionally tripping and falling headlong, until he neared the canal. He made his way carefully down the stones lining the sloping walls of the canal and stepped to the edge of the water, then dove in headfirst. Swimming like a frog, he made his way to the other side of the canal, then dragged himself halfway out of the water and listened. Hearing nothing but his pounding heart and gasping breath, he clambered up the wall of the canal and lurched toward the home of the only person who would receive him and help him now.

As the young man approached his place of refuge, his strength gave out and he collapsed noisily against the front door in a heap.

The wife of Amel-labashi bolted upright in bed and shook her husband by the arm. "Amel," she hissed in the dark, "someone is trying to break into our home!"

Among the tribes and clans that had settled in and around Babylon, Amel-labashi was recognized as a spokesman for those who remained loyal to El Shaddai, the Creator, the God of Father Adam and Father Noah.

Rising immediately from his bed, Amel rushed to the front door of his home, donning a tunic as he went. Hearing no other sounds, he raised the latch on the door and turned the handle. An unseen weight forced the door open and an unconscious body flopped over the threshold. Peering up and down the street and seeing no one, Amel-labashi stretched the body out on the ground outside his home and called for his wife, En-nigaldi, to light a lamp. She first lit a taper in the fireplace, then used it to light a small bronze lamp, which she brought to the door.

Holding the light over the young man's face, Amel peered closely, then looked up at his nervous wife. "It's Reza," he said, "the son of Zakir the brick-maker."

"Bring him inside." En-nigaldi said. "Clean him up while I get some clean clothes."

The sun was already up when Reza awoke, as if from a fitful nightmare, and sat up on a sleeping mat in a strange room. He looked around the room and noticed personal items belonging to children. He could see that whoever took him in must have moved their children out to make room for him. He got up and stepped quickly to the door and peered out. Seeing En-nigaldi talking with a servant down the hall, and knowing her to be the wife of Amel-labashi, Reza closed the door, relieved that he had made it to a safe place after all. He was not ready to talk to anyone yet; first he had to sort things out from the night before.

Reza sat down on his sleeping mat, rubbed his eyes, and wondered, "Did it really happen? Was it just a bad dream?" Then the events of the previous night began to play through his mind.

His preparation for initiation into the new religion began with purification rituals. He was told by the priests that he must purify himself before approaching the gods, the spirit masters. With this in mind, Reza fasted for three days, taking only water. He was also made to swear under oath that he had not had intimate relations in at least four weeks. He protested, declaring that he was a virgin, which delighted the priests.

The purification process also included a time of confession in a darkened room surrounded by priests who looked very ominous and threatening to Reza. He felt as though he were on trial before judges. He was forced to reveal every secret thing in his life, every sinful deed, every sinful thought he had ever had, all the way back to his early childhood. Reza could not help but think that he had already confessed his sins to El Shaddai, who had forgiven him. His father, Zakir, had made the required sacrifices for the family's sins. "How was it," he wondered, "that *men* had the power or authority to forgive sins?"

After the confession, Reza was taken into a small room, in the center of which was a large bronze tub filled with water. The priests ordered him to strip and step into the water, which Reza did, hesitatingly. He was disturbed at the way the priests leered at him. They then closed in around him. After instructing Reza to kneel down, a ritual priest, a *mashmashu*, raised a pitcher of water and poured it over him, chanting mysterious incantations.

The other priests took branches from the hyssop plant and used them to scrub Reza's body. Then they ordered him to step out of the tub, whereupon they dried him and anointed his body with fragrant oils. Reza was most uncomfortable with this. He felt he was somehow being violated.

After the ritual bath, Reza was dressed in a clean white robe and a wreath made with narrow, pointed palm leaves was placed on his head. The ends of the leaves pointed outward from the center, like rays emanating from the sun.

As the *mashmashu* chanted in a bizarre tongue, another priest approached Reza and blindfolded him. A long silence ensued, where the only thing Reza could hear was his gasping breath. Finally, an eerie, other-worldly voice whispered in his ear, making his heart stop and his hair stand on end. The non-human voice said "The goal for those who attain the secret knowledge is godhood! You shall become a *god!*"

Stunned, Reza was then led, or rather jerked along, by a piece of cloth wrapped around his neck. He stumbled along winding hallways and up and down stairs for what seemed like an eternity. He only knew it was the middle of the night and he really should have been at home resting comfortably on his bed, dreaming of Vashti.

Vashti! What would she think of him *now?* Would he ever hold her in his arms again and see her beautiful face looking up at him?

Finally, Reza felt soft earth under his feet and felt the cool night air on his face. He was outside, but where, and why? An answer, of sorts, soon came. The blindfold was removed and as Reza's eyes adjusted to the night he saw that at his feet lay an open grave!

Before he could respond, an attendant approached with a torch, and Reza could see a goat nearby, tethered to a stake in the ground. As Reza watched, terrified, a priest slit the goat's throat, and grasping the dying animal by the scruff of its neck, began to drain its blood into a bowl.

Several men grabbed Reza and bound his wrists and ankles. He was turned around, bewildered and terrified, with his back to the open grave. The *mashmashu* approached Reza and stared into his face. The priest's eyes seemed to blaze and his face took on a hideous and threatening appearance. There was a presence, a spirit, rising from within the priest, becoming larger than the priest, looming over and around him. Reza sensed it more than saw it. A horrifying thought raced through his mind: 'This is who they are worshipping! The beings are real, but they are evil!'

The priest raised the bowl of goat's blood over Reza's head and poured it over him, chanting loudly, "Having thus died, you arise reborn, eternal, begotten by the goddess. You are the divine consort of Ishtar, for having attained the forbidden knowledge, you have become a god!"

Reza was then pushed into the grave, landing hard on his back, and as he screamed, dirt was shoveled in, quickly covering him.

Reza now fought like a trapped animal. Twisting and writhing furiously, he managed to get one foot free of the rope that bound his ankles. Rising to his feet, he leaped out of the grave like a bloodied zombie and whirled around in a panic. A priest lunged for him, and Reza swung his arms, still bound at the wrists, like a club, catching the priest under the chin and sending him sailing backward, landing on the stake where the unfortunate goat was tied. The priest rolled over with a deep gasping sigh, then lay still. Blood oozed from a deep gash in his back.

The rest of the priests formed a circle, menacingly, around Reza. He kicked one of the priests in the stomach, causing him to double over in pain. Then, running to a nearby gate, he kicked it open, stepped outside, then turned to defend himself once more.

As a priestly attendant ran through the gate, Reza clubbed him across the face, knocking him into the brick wall. The next person coming through the gate was the *mashmashu* himself. Reza swung his right foot with all his might, catching the *mashmashu* between the legs; he dropped to the ground like a rock and folded up into a fetal position, groaning. A knife slipped from his hand onto the dirt.

Reza did not wait any longer. He turned and fled for his life.

Returning to the present, Reza knelt on his sleeping mat in the bedroom in Amel-labashi's home, facing the window. The morning sun shined reassuringly into the room. Reza gazed in wonder at the infinitely tiny particles of dust that slowly drifted through the white beam of sunlight that penetrated the room.

Lifting his thoughts to God he began to pray: "El Shaddai, Father God, God of my ancestors, forgive me for turning away from you in my rebellious pride. Forgive me for seeking a way of spirituality that is not authorized or blessed by you. Thank you Father for sparing me and warning me in time, and not letting me be lost. I ask for forgiveness and restoration with you and my loved ones. Thank you Father. I will never be unfaithful to you again. Help me to be strong. Oh, El Shaddai, I almost forgot something; if it's your will, please give me Vashti to be my wife."

Rising to his feet, with his burden of guilt removed, Reza opened the door to the bedroom and went into the dining area of his hosts' home. At the table sat Amel-labashi and his wife En-nigaldi, both of whom looked up at Reza solemnly as he entered the room. Amel-labashi motioned for Reza to sit down.

"You owe us an explanation, young man." said Amel. "I'll get something for him to eat," murmured En-nigaldi rising. Casting a stern glance back at Reza, she added, "Your poor mother! And that poor, precious girl, Vashti! Hmmpf!" She walked away shaking her head.

Reza turned and looked sheepishly at Amel-labashi.

"Well?" said Amel with arched eyebrows. "Speak, son."

CHAPTER TWENTY

Nimrod's Oration

D ays six through ten of the New Year Festival continued as the preceding days had, except that the drinking, dancing, and carousing were spinning out of control and were taking a toll on the people. Sex acts were occurring in public, in broad daylight, regardless of onlookers. Theft and robbery were rampant. Children were neglected or abused. The spirits in the vortex exulted as people bowed and worshipped their idols and praised the names of the false gods, while the true Heavenly Father and Creator grieved over the wrong choices of his children. He would not force them to love him, for love must be the act of a free will.

Even the king and the priests realized that the situation in Babylon had gotten out of hand and that public order must be restored. So on the evening of the tenth day of the festival a royal proclamation was issued that the following day, day eleven, was to be a day of fasting and penance and that the people should remain in their homes.

Only stray dogs and cats could be seen on the streets of Babylon as that day of penance, and much needed recuperation, lazily passed.

However, on day twelve, the final day of the festival, excitement ran high as the king, gloriously arrayed, was paraded through the city on a throne carried by porters, with an idol of Marduk carried next to him. Nimrod's face and hands were powdered with gold dust, giving him the brilliant countenance of a deity. As king and idol, presented as gods, were carried up the Processional Way to the Ishtar Gate, the king's hand rested on the hand of Marduk and the people fell down to worship both king and god.

Observing this, the high priest turned to a scribe and said, "This will be part of the New Year Festival from now on. The king shall 'take the hand of Marduk'!"

Passing through the Ishtar Gate, leaving the City, the procession made an abrupt left turn, then turned left again at the river and marched down the roadway between the city wall and the Euphrates River. A huge crowd followed the procession while thousands flowed through the Sacred Precinct or climbed up on the city wall to watch the spectacle. Thousands more lined both banks of the Euphrates.

Upon reaching the bridge that spanned the river Nimrod stepped down from his throne which was then set on a raised platform facing the crowds and the entrance to the Sacred Precinct. He then turned to the people and with a fierce, arrogant look on his radiant face sat down enthroned as a god. He raised his hand and waited for the people to become silent.

As a hush fell across the mob, Nimrod the Rebel began to speak, with a voice that seemed unnaturally amplified.

"I am Nimrod, ancestor of Cush, Ham, and Noah. I am called 'the Rebel' and a 'Hunter of Men' for that is what I am, and I come from a line of rebels. As our ancestor Ham rebelled against the authority of his father Noah, who lay drunk and naked in his tent, and as Ham's sons Cush, Mizraim, and Canaan likewise rebelled against all authority, even so do I follow in their ways.

"However, I, your king, have a greater task than those who came before us. They stood proud and defiant against human authority, while I, Nimrod, stand against the supposed God of all creation! This God, this nameless, faceless God that some call El Shaddai — God Almighty — gave mankind the command to 'fill the whole earth'. By this he meant to scatter and weaken us! He fears that we will assert ourselves and neglect him. And that is what man *will* do, under my leadership! Your peace, happiness, and prosperity flow not from God but from me and our Lord Marduk!"

At this the crowds wavered a moment, hesitatingly, then raised a great cheer.

Unseen by the people, the great dark vortex cloud poised above their city moved and repositioned itself over the ominous tower facing the Temple of Marduk.

To the eye capable of multi-dimensional vision, the great tiered pyramid tower with the whirling vortex above it looked like a pair of dark triangles, one inverted above the other. The apexes of the triangles almost touched, like the upper and lower parts of an hourglass.

In the midst of the vortex Chulgomet cried out, "As above, so below!"

A thunderous roar of victory erupted from the host of fallen spirits.

What was taking place in the spirit realm was having its physical manifestation in the human realm.

Nimrod's attack on God continued.

"I declare vengeance on God," the king raged, "for almost completely destroying mankind in the Great Flood — a cowardly, deceitful deed. He punishes those who assert their independence. He wreaks vengeance on those who would be gods.

"Listen, my people. It is cowardice to submit to God! We will exalt ourselves and the gods of our own choosing! For this reason we honor Marduk. And, as you know, even Marduk has a lord — Lucifer the Bringer of Light! It was he who said to Mother Eve and Father Adam, 'For God knows that on the day you eat of the fruit of the tree of the knowledge of good and evil, your eyes will be opened and *you shall be as gods!*'"

Nimrod raised his arms skyward and cried out, "We *have* tasted this fruit, our eyes *are* opened, and we *shall* be as gods!"

The king's mad boast provoked an immediate roar of approval from the crowd.

"I, Nimrod, have subjected all peoples to myself. I am their lord. I am the right arm of Marduk. As your lord I am building the mighty tower that faces Marduk's temple. I call this great edifice *Etemen-anki,* the 'House of the Foundation of Heaven and Earth'! And by this great structure, which I raise in defiance of the supposed God Almighty, I will draw all gods and all peoples together in unity!"

The king stood and gestured toward the span of the Euphrates River bridge behind him and declared "I am the *Pontifex Maximus,* the 'Supreme Bridge-Keeper'! This will be my title and that of my successors through the ages, for I am, and they will be, the mediators between gods and men.

"I am your god on Earth, your savior, and your mediator!"

The crowd again roared its approval, while Nimrod basked in glory.

The *sa anga* and the other priests stared aghast at the king.

Nimrod shifted his gaze to the top of the tower Etemen-anki. 'Is there something there, above the tower?' he wondered.

Not seeing anything unusual, Nimrod nonetheless had an image impressed on his mind. As he stood staring, immobilized, the shape of the pyramid tower, with an upside down triangular image of the vortex above it, was etched in his mind. His lips parted as he uttered words he did not understand.

"As above, so below."

⇢⊜ CHAPTER TWENTY-ONE ⊜⇠

False Messiahs and the Queen of Heaven

I n another dimension, a meeting of rebel spirit lords came to order.

"This meeting of the Supreme Strategy Council is now in session" Chulgomet declared. "We have present with us the lords Ishtar, Baal-zebub, Asmodeus, Baphomet, Pu Satanakia, Valafar, Sargatanos, Belial, Pruslas, Vasago, Aamon, and of course, Marduk.

"Our Lord Lucifer bids us meet to review our progress with the humans and their rebel leaders, Nimrod and Semiramis, and to plot future strategy."

Chulgomet glanced around at his fellow spirits and said, "Any comments before we proceed?"

Ishtar spoke, "Nimrod's independence is disturbing." A murmur of agreement went up.

Chulgomet replied hastily, "We will address that issue Lord Ishtar. It is on our agenda.

"As you are aware, my lords," he continued, "the Creator attempted to make a ruin of our work by destroying humanity in the Great Flood. He failed didn't he! It was a great set-back, but we have recovered.

"God commanded the humans who survived to multiply and fill the Earth, but we have raised up leaders, a ruthless man and woman, who have corralled the human beasts into an empire under our control. We have successfully channeled to them a religion of our own design. We are their gods and we have them groveling before our idols, even sacrificing their children in the fire to us!"

Chulgomet looked down and shook his head, snickering.

"The fools don't realize it is we they are communicating with when they channel with spirits. The *goood* angels only communicate with humans at God's bidding, never when humans summon them! Never! Oh my, the goood angels are sooo obeeeedient," Chulgomet sneered derisively. "They would never, ever, use their own initiative!

"Humans! They are so easily deceived, and it's so entertaining!"

Chuckling with delight, Chulgomet addressed one of his fellows. "Lord Baphomet, will you update this Council on the status of the human priesthood? Oh, and Baphomet, why on Earth do the humans depict you with a goat's head?"

"My chosen symbol is the pentagram, Lord Chulgomet," replied Baphomet obligingly. "It's an inverted five-pointed star. If you look closely at a goat's head with its horns, ears, and chin, you will see the shape of the pentagram. I also find it quite entertaining to occupy one of the loathsome goat creatures and wander amongst the humans making hideous noises and smells!"

After a long uncomfortable silence Chulgomet replied slowly, "We, um, all find ways to entertain ourselves."

"Ahem, now Colleagues," Baphomet began again, "our mission to spiritually corrupt the human animals was initiated with the woman, Semiramis, per Lord Lucifer's instructions. She has been absolutely cooperative has she not, Lord Marduk?"

Marduk's face contorted into a leering, salacious grin that sent laughter through the assembly.

"Through her," Baphomet explained, "we have instituted a priesthood to lead the rest of the humans astray. The priests are those who have rejected the Creator and desire to rise above and dominate their fellowmen. The priests have yielded themselves to us directly, in exchange for knowledge and a sense of energizing power that we give them. But do not be concerned; they are pets on leashes and don't realize it.

"We have instituted initiation rituals by channeling them to Queen Semiramis," Baphomet continued. "The initiations are designed to discourage or frighten away the thrill seekers, the faint-hearted, and the stupid, while allowing strong-willed individuals to rise into higher and higher levels of hidden knowledge and power. They are bound at each new level with stronger and more terrible oaths and threats. Secrecy is guaranteed by the torture and death of themselves and their loved ones. And Colleagues — you will appreciate this — the symbols and rituals of our initiations mock and mimic those that God plans to institute among the humans at a later time!"

"Thank you Lord Baphomet," said Chulgomet. "Baal-zebub — Lord of the Flies — would you review our plans for human sexuality and the marriage relationship?"

"Of course!" said Baal-zebub, seething with resentment over Chulgomet's use of his nickname, which he deeply despised. "The Creator's intention, from the beginning, is that a man and woman should leave their parents and join themselves to each other in a lifelong relationship as husband and wife. God even says that, in that relationship, they will become one flesh. We are not certain what he means by that, but it seems to relate to some higher relationship between the future Messiah/Savior we have heard of, and the people who will be his own. He will be 'in them' and they will be 'in him', or some such blather.

"It matters not," Baal-zebub said carelessly. "If the husband/wife relationship is of such great importance to God and humans, then we must destroy it by any and every means! This is best accomplished through sexual infidelity — adultery! Why, the very word means to make impure through mixture. When the husband or wife turns to someone outside of their marriage relationship for sexual gratification, they have broken the bond and the purity of their God-ordained union! They are no longer one flesh! The relationship is thus weakened and dissolves, along with the family unit itself. When the family structure is weakened chaos will run rampant through human societies like a plague, and the ones who deserve to suffer least — the children — will be the ones who suffer most.

"Concerning sex, our strategy must always be to make human sexuality as animalistic as possible! We must deceive them into thinking that sex is of no more consequence than scratching an itch! Little do they know that, for them, sex is a river of fire that must be banked and cooled by a hundred restraints if it is not to consume them and wreck their lives, their families, and their societies!

"We know," continued Baal-zebub, "that the male humans are much, much more visually oriented than the females are, much more excited by what their eyes behold. They also tend be more adventurous. Therefore, our strategy should be the physical enticement of married men by women who are not their wives.

Erotic artwork and images can also draw them into lustful and shameful activities.

"Once the hook is in, the men can be led like cattle into all kinds of harmful and ruinous situations. Why, a decent man's reputation, built up by a lifetime of honest living, can be wrecked in a moment by a single sexual indiscretion!

"Colleagues," Baal-zebub said excitedly, "we know that God's design for the family unit, consisting of a father, a mother, and their children, is fundamental to human security and well-being, not to mention the overall integrity and cohesiveness of their societies. Whatever we can do to disrupt the family unit will promote chaos and a breakdown in morality, both of which serve our purposes. For it is in the midst of such confusion and insecurity that we may rule over their lives.

"Finally," he concluded, "the Creator's intention is that each man be the priest of his own family, the spiritual head of every home. We have not had to do much of anything to discourage that! They simply ignore God's command. That makes it easy for our own priesthood to take over that vital function!"

"Thank you Baal-zebub," said Chulgomet. "Oh, and sorry for the bit about 'Lord of the Flies'! That was most inappropriate in a gathering such as this."

Baal-zebub fumed. Was this an apology or salt in the wound?

Chulgomet continued, "Colleagues, you have just heard reference to the future Messiah of God. As we have discussed previously it seems that God himself will take human form as a savior and redeemer of the humans. As astonishing as it sounds, he intends to make a way for the wretched human creatures to be made holy and completely reconciled with himself!

"And now Lord Belial has additional information for us concerning this all-important issue."

Belial spoke smoothly, "While we don't fully comprehend the Creator's intention concerning this Messiah, the 'Anointed One', we may surmise that he will be an exceedingly powerful being. We have even received information to the effect that he will someday wield an iron scepter over us! If there is any truth to this then we must take offensive action to undo his effectiveness. If masses of humans can be deceived and led astray concerning God's truth, before it is revealed, then they will not recognize it when it comes!"

"That bears repeating," Chulgomet interjected. "Did you hear it Colleagues? I'll repeat it myself, "'If humans can be deceived and led astray concerning God's truth, before it is revealed, then they will not recognize it when it comes.'"

"Brilliant, Lord Belial!" Chulgomet exulted. "I believe you have laid bare one of our Lord Lucifer's central strategies! We must work ahead of God, using deception and confusion, to undo his plans before they come to be! Then, when this Messiah makes his appearance, he will discover that he is just one of many messiahs! In fact, he will be a late comer, for the tribes and nations will already have their messiahs!"

At this, Chulgomet roared with satisfaction and said, "Continue, Belial."

"Thank you, Lord Chulgomet. Our Lord Lucifer is the wisest of all beings! Utilizing his strategy, Colleagues, we anticipate God combining the high priestly and kingly functions in one person. We expect this to be manifested in this Messiah, God's Anointed One, who is somehow God himself. Outrageous isn't it? Knowing this, we have bestowed these functions on our man Nimrod, as Pontifex Maximus, with instructions to continue them through his successors through the ages, where ever humans live. When God's Shepherd King arrives he will bring nothing new to mankind!"

"Excellent!" Chulgomet exclaimed. "And now Lord Asmodeus will enlighten us concerning other aspects of the Messiah's advent."

Asmodeus moved in front of the assembly with his head bowed low, then slowly raised his head, and with an evil countenance and wicked words began to speak. "Colleagues, it may interest you to know that we have new information, direct from Lord Lucifer's throne, that only Lord Chulgomet and myself are privy to. We have learned much about the Messiah to come, and it directly affects us all."

All eyes were now riveted on Asmodeus.

"We know, Colleagues, that God is...is...*love,* that detestable word! But he is also holy and he is just. His holiness and sense of justice means that he will not and cannot allow sin to go unpunished. It would be contradictory to his nature to do so. This is a burden *we* must bear. But those frail human beasts have free wills even as we do, and since they have free wills, and choose to sin, it means that they are separated from God as well! And since it is not in them to be able to measure up to God's standards of righteousness and holiness, they need a savior whether they know it or not!"

Asmodeus leaned forward, his eyes penetrating his listeners.

"Here is the crucial point: from God's perspective, sin must be punished. It must be atoned for. He is not like a doting, permissive human grandfather who dismisses sin with a chuckle and a wave of his hand. So, if he gives every man what he deserves, there would be no one left to love God or to worship him, for all have sinned.

"What to do?" he queried. "Put the punishment they deserve on *someone else*! Put it on someone who *is* righteous and has lived up to God's holy standards and therefore does not deserve punishment. Then, Colleagues, God's justice is satisfied, the sins of the humans are forgiven, with God's character intact, and the humans are not destroyed. Not only that, but they are restored to fellowship with him, fellowship as we once had with him!"

"In other words," intoned Chulgomet, "a once and for all substitutionary sacrifice will remove God's judgment for those who are covered by it."

"Precisely!" agreed Asmodeus. "The practice was begun with Adam, and continued through Noah and his sons, to bring an animal to the altar as a blood sacrifice. The problem with that is it must be done over and over again. Sin must be removed by an atoning blood sacrifice. For as we all are aware..." At this point every member of the Council repeated the words like bored schoolchildren. 'Without the shedding of blood there is no forgiveness of sins!'"

"Yes!" cried Asmodeus, "and this task of continually having to make sacrifice for sin is, itself, a tedious burden to the humans and the practice has almost died out."

Sargatanos spoke up, "I would say we have corrupted the practice and made it detestable in the Creator's sight."

"Yes, the smell of human flesh must be a stench in the Creator's nose!" added Pu Satanakia.

"You are both quite correct," replied Marduk. "How satisfying, to take the things of God and pervert them so they accomplish the opposite of what he intended!"

"And that is what we will do," added Asmodeus, "regarding this Messiah that God intends to send, who will take away the sins of all who are identified with him by faith.

"We will send counterfeit messiahs," shouted Chulgomet, "starting with Nimrod!"

"Nimrod must be sacrificed," interjected the spirit lord Pruslas, "and be declared the savior and redeemer of the people!"

"But God's Messiah cannot remain in the grave to rot like other human animals," said Vasago. "He must rise from death!"

"And he will! cried Chulgomet. "The humans must be taught that our messiahs will also return from the dead."

"But we cannot accomplish that, Chulgomet," Belial pointed out. We can kill, but we cannot give life. Our messiahs will be proven false."

Pu Satanakia joined the fray. "Colleagues," he shouted, "there is a way out of this dilemma. While it is true that we cannot raise our messiahs from the dead, the teaching should be spread among our cults and religions that the savior's return is to be expected by his being literally born again to some special, sanctified woman."

"A 'Queen of Heaven!'" several spirits shouted at once.

"Semiramis will be the first!" declared Chulgomet.

Asmodeus jumped in. "If God is going to become like one of the humans, as their Savior, then it follows that he, even he, will be born into human flesh as a baby!"

"This cannot be!" cried Belial, unable to believe what he was hearing. "The Creator of the universe... *a human baby!* You are all insane!"

"It's insane but it must be!" roared Chulgomet. "It would be meaningless for God, as God, to fulfill his own requirements for righteousness. How could he impute that righteousness to humans? No, the punishment for sin must be placed on a man who has satisfied God's requirements for holiness while at the same time being subject to the sufferings and frailties that every human faces, but without sin. He will not deserve God's judgment but will accept it anyway. And by so doing, receives in himself the punishment for sin that was reserved for others. This is why humans require a savior. They cannot save themselves!

"Proceed, Asmodeus" said Chulgomet, struggling to steady himself.

"Well then, we agree on our enemy's strategy," Asmodeus stated emphatically. "The True Messiah is to die a sacrificial death for the sins of humanity and whoever becomes identified with this atoning sacrifice, by faith, shares in the Messiah's righteousness and is forgiven of their sins, thereby reconciling them with God and establishing them as his children."

Even as the words left his mouth, the entire assembly rose as one and erupted in a screaming rage of opposition to the Creator's plan of redemption.

Asmodeus patiently allowed the riot to subside, then continued.

"This being the case my lords, our master Lucifer has directed us to dilute the effectiveness of the Messiah by raising up false messiahs before the real one makes his appearance. Nimrod will be the first of many such messiahs. We will raise them up wherever humans live. What each instance will have in common is the idea, false of course, that the alleged messiah, having died, will return to save the people by being born again to what we are already calling a Queen of Heaven. Since Nimrod is to become the first false messiah, his queen, Semiramis, will become the first Queen of Heaven!"

Chulgomet intervened in a loud voice. "This is the model, the prototype! We will instigate teachings, legends, artwork, songs, and drama that describe a hero who dies and is to return through rebirth as a child to save and redeem the people from their sins. We will raise up messiahs under many different names and titles — saviors, heroes, gods, demi-gods, warrior kings, avatars — but whatever they are called by the people, their purpose is to draw humanity away from the true Messiah, and to dilute the importance of his revelation!"

Chulgomet concluded the meeting of the Supreme Strategy Council. "This image of the holy mother and child is to be known and worshipped and adored wherever humans are found. This directive comes from our Lord Lucifer. He has determined that this image will distract the people from God, and when the True Messiah is revealed he will find that he is just one of many!

"Nimrod will be our first messiah. He must die a sacrificial death, for the sins of the people! Yes, he will save the people from their sins! Or so we will teach them. Now, that leaves an issue unresolved: Semiramis must become pregnant after her husband dies."

"That will not be difficult to arrange, Lord Chulgomet!" cried Baal-zebub. "Is there not already a man who guards her private chamber, whom she beds with when the King is away?"

CHAPTER TWENTY-TWO

Eshnunna

The king's hands clenched into fists as rage rose into his face. A trembling baldheaded scribe stood before him reading words etched on clay tablets, just delivered from the city of Eshnunna.

The scribe was loath to disturb the king during his afternoon rest, but the palace administrator, Itti-balatu, became alarmed when the scribe read the message to him and immediately escorted him to the king's private chambers. Pushing the frightened scribe into the king's quarters, Itti-balatu quickly closed the door and waited outside.

The scribe, named Shuma-ukin, now faced the king's wrath. Nimrod spun about and took two steps toward the window of his chamber and stopped with his back to the scribe. With his hands on his hips and his head tilted back, staring at the ceiling, the king enunciated his words slowly.

"Read that to me again scribe. I must not have understood you properly. Read carefully and make no mistakes, for the consequences of this message could be quite drastic for the people of Eshnunna."

The terrified scribe read the message again.

ilshu-iliya, Chief Elder of Eshnunna
To Ninus, King of Babylon

Greetings in the Name of our God,
El Shaddai, the only God, Creator
of everything that is, the Keeper of
our souls.

We, the elders of Eshnunna, have
received the correspondence
from you regarding the imposition
of an annual levy of gold, silver,
livestock, and our agricultural
produce. You have also requisitioned
the service of our young men in the
king's army.

Please know that Eshnunna is a hard-
working and self-sustaining community.
However, the city has fallen on difficult
times. It may have come to the king's
attention that Eshnunna has experienced
drought conditions for two growing seasons.
As a result, the city's primary canal, the
Ahwaz canal, dried up last summer.
This unfortunate event has had a devas-

tating effect on the city's barley, date, and
fig harvests, as well as on the production
of hay and other feed for our livestock.

The king must understand that at this time
Eshnunna can barely feed itself. Our reserves

of gold and silver have already been bartered
with outsiders for grain and olive oil.

The Council of Elders also expresses its
horror and dismay at the news of the king's
vicious and unprovoked attacks on other
towns and villages, resulting in the inexcusable
destruction of human life which only El Shaddai
has the right to take. Even more alarming,
is the king's apparent rejection of the only
true god, El Shaddai, in favor of such gods
as Marduk, Ishtar, Shammash, and Nebu
who are not gods at all, only imposters!

The King's requirement that Eshnunna construct
a temple to Marduk, and institute his worship there,
is utterly rejected by the council and the citizens.

We also reject the king's aggression and unfairness
in making demands of levy and tribute which the city
desperately needs for the sustenance of its own
citizens.

We stand in solidarity with our brothers and sisters,
the Babylonians, and will as always, beseech the
blessing of God Almighty, El Shaddai, for you all.

"Aaaaaaghh!!!" Nimrod whirled around in a blind fury. Seeing
a fruit bowl on a table nearby, he snatched it and threw it in the
direction of Shuma-ukin.

Realizing in a split second that to duck or turn and flee could
result in the loss of his life, the scribe simply stood, immobile, as

the ceramic fruit bowl struck him in the face and shattered.

At that moment two men peeked sheepishly from the door to the king's chamber. It was the palace administrator, Itti-balatu, and the king's aide Arioch.

Spying them, Nimrod nodded toward the scribe, Shuma-ukin, who now laid bloodied on the floor, and said to the administrator, "Get him out of here and clean him up." And to Arioch he said, "Summon the generals. We have another rebellious city to deal with!"

Nimrod rode at the head of his army as it passed through the Ishtar Gate at the northern end of the City of Babylon, then turned slightly to the northeast toward Eshnunna, some 90 miles away.

Just a few miles outside the City of Babylon, he stopped to observe the work of his engineers and surveyors as they laid out the boundaries of what was to become Babylon's sister city.

From the earliest times the southern part of Nimrod's kingdom, where the ancient people called the Sumerians had lived, had been known in the Babylonian tongue as Ki-Enki, or Land of Enki, the patriarchal god of the Sumerians. Nimrod's heart and soul, as well as his cultural identity, derived from that land, and he saw his city, Babylon, as its new capital. However, the northern part of Nimrod's kingdom was known as Akkad, and it was part of the King's long-range plan to construct a sister city to Babylon that would also serve as the administrative capital of his northern kingdom. Accordingly, it would be called Akkad City. Slave laborers and civil servants stood at attention as Nimrod and his soldiers passed by.

Nimrod's soldiers were lean and rugged. It was nothing for them to arise before the sun and jog at a forced pace for hours on end through the heat of the day and into the night. Then, after a few of hours sleep, get up and do it again the next day. Nimrod and his generals slept on the ground like the common foot soldiers, albeit in separate tents. Everyone observed the same rules, ate the same food, and did without the company of females, until victory was celebrated, then woe indeed to the women and girls who were found alive.

But, unlike the unfortunate citizens of Dur Sharukkin, the people of Eshnunna were preparing themselves for the onslaught to come. Anticipating a violent response from Nimrod, the council of elders ordered the Eshnunnaites to dig a ditch around their city and construct behind it an inner fortified wall of stones and rubble.

Lacking sufficient time and resources to manufacture proper weapons of war, which the locals were unfamiliar with anyway, they had nonetheless collected every type of farm implement and artisan's tool that could be found. With these, and with bows and arrows the people used for hunting, the elders armed a hastily organized and clumsily outfitted militia. Finally, scouts were dispatched to keep watch for Nimrod's forces.

The people of Eshnunna now prayed and waited.

Two days outside of Eshnunna, several of Nimrod's hunters surprised a small group of scouts sent by the council of elders. In the skirmish that ensued, two of the three scouts were killed, while the third escaped and fled back to Eshnunna.

"They know we're coming," spat Nimrod as he knelt in his tent to discuss strategy with his generals. "The element of surprise has been removed."

"True, my Lord Ninus," replied General Nebu-zaradan, "but our forces number two thousand and two hundred men, whereas our sources estimate that there are only some six hundred to seven hundred fighting men in Eshnunna."

"And poorly armed and trained," added General Nergal-shahrezer.

Nebu-zaradan continued, "They cannot withstand a frontal assault, followed by our lancers and chariots."

"It will be like slaughtering sheep," chuckled General Marduk-sarsekim. The general was known as *Nebu*-sarsekim until the elevation of the god Marduk to supreme status. He then decided it was politically advantageous to change his name.

"A simple exercise for the men! Nothing more!" he said.

Nimrod grunted in agreement with his generals. He then looked up at his aide Arioch. "Call the diviners and fortune-tellers. I want to know what the omens are; what do the gods say?"

Arioch bowed and left the tent.

Nimrod turned back to his generals, "Surely the omens and the gods will agree with me, that the day after tomorrow is the day to attack!" he said, grinning.

The generals laughed and slapped one another on the back. "Like slaughtering sheep! A rabbit hunt!" they repeated.

In the present situation Nimrod abandoned his policy of secret attack, for in this case his opponent knew of his intentions and his whereabouts. But he held to his policy of dividing the opposing forces to prevent a unified defense. So during the early pre-dawn hours on the morning of battle the king ordered half of his troops to the other side of Eshnunna under generals Marduk-sarsekim and Nergal-shahrezer so the attack would commence simultaneously from two sides of the city. The remainder of the troops, under generals Nebu-zaradan and Nebu-shazdan, were positioned directly in front of the entrance to the city. On order of the generals bonfires were lit at spaced intervals in a ring around the city.

On a rocky hilltop overlooking the city stood Nimrod with his aides and diviners. In his mind, the king visualized the destruction and carnage soon to begin. His heart pounded with excitement and bloodlust. He began to pray aloud to Marduk.

"In your name O' Marduk, I wreak vengeance on our enemies! Give us victory this day!"

"Ayaaaah!" cried a young priest, adding his blessing to the king's petition. "O' goddess Ishtar," he cried out, "Mistress of the gods, Lioness, Queen of the battle, supporter of arms! Where you gaze, the dead live and the living die! Give us victory this day O' Queen of bloodshed, for we are your servants!"

Despite these urgent requests something entirely unexpected was occurring on the other side of Eshnunna.

General Marduk-sarsekim and General Nergal-shahrezer were leading their troops, numbering some eight hundred men, through a narrow canyon toward the edge of the city. Oblivious to the possibility of a pre-emptive strike from the Eshnunnaites, the troops trudged along in the early morning darkness with their weapons put away.

Just a rabbit hunt.

A shout from above them shattered the morning stillness.

"Now!"

A split second later a man-made landslide of rocks and boulders came crashing down upon the Babylonian troops. A shower of arrows rained down upon the soldiers that struggled to respond. As groaning, shouting men thrashed about in the dark canyon, buckets of flaming kerosene were pitched on them by their unseen Eshnunnaite attackers.

Also unseen were the fallen spirits observing the situation.

"Perfect!" cried Chulgomet gleefully. "The innocent are responding with violence! This must be reported to Lucifer!"

"Violence begets violence," said Baal-zebub, nodding with smug satisfaction.

A bloodlust had now overcome the normally peaceful men of Eshnunna as they mercilessly bombarded the Babylonian soldiers with stones, arrows, and flaming kerosene. What choice did they have? The lives of their wives and children, as well as their own lives, were in mortal danger. If they did nothing they would all die horrible deaths.

A new mindset was becoming ingrained in the collective consciousness of humankind:

> *Violence must be met with violence;*
> *passivity means death;*
> *appeasement is weakness;*
> *kill the other man before he kills you.*

The whole creation began to groan like a woman in labor.

The Babylonian soldiers in the canyon were recovering their equilibrium now, and their archers were finding their targets. The attackers became the prey as stricken Eshnunnaites fell mortally wounded onto the rocks below.

Realizing they were greatly outnumbered, and that the Babylonians were rallying for a counteroffensive, the surviving Eshnunnaites withdrew and fled back into their city to join their brothers.

At a blast of horns from Nimrod's hilltop command post, the siege of Eshnunna began.

The men and boys of Eshnunna stood at their posts at the fortified wall and stared dumbfounded and open-mouthed as hundreds of raging, cursing soldiers charged at them from the darkness surrounding their city.

What had they done to deserve *this*?

The main body of the Babylonian army was about to find out, however, that this was to be no rabbit hunt.

As the attackers neared the city they had to cross the ditch in front of the fortified wall. In the darkness they could not see the black, sticky substance that covered the bottom of the ditch. Nor, in the noise and tumult of the moment, did they pay notice to the oily stench rising from the muck they were plodding through.

The defenders of Eshnunna now raised flame-tipped arrows and shot them into the ditch surrounding their city. A massive wall of flames erupted instantly, along with the piercing screams of hundreds of human torches.

Watching from his command post Nimrod at first laughed out loud at the sight of human fireballs tumbling and rolling in the dark fields below him. However, his laughter stopped abruptly as he realized it was *his* soldiers that were being burned alive.

Laughter now turned to rage.

Nimrod turned on a hapless messenger standing nearby and

shouted in his face. "Tell generals Shazdan and Zaradan to make a bridge across the ditch! Use men's bodies if necessary!"

The king sputtered in his rage, "Breach that wall, kill everyone! Spare no one, not even the babies, or the animals!"

The king whirled around looking for an aide, "Shapik-zeri!" he yelled frantically.

A young messenger stepped forward.

"Awaiting your orders Lord Ninus," he said, bowing and raising his folded hands in front of his face.

Nimrod addressed the young man. "Marduk-sarsekim and Nergal-shahrezer should be approaching the far side of the city by now. Go to them immediately and tell them to raise a bridge over the ditch, using whatever materials are available, even corpses. They are to breach the defensive wall and destroy everything that breathes."

"Yes my Lord," replied Shapik-zeri, as he turned to his task.

The sun was now rising and Nimrod could see that his men were beginning to clamber over the crude defensive perimeter that had been erected against them. Once inside the wall, the simple peasant folk of Eshnunna were no match for the king's warriors.

Peering across to the far side of the city, Nimrod could see that some of Nergal-shahrezer and Marduk-sarsekim's men were fighting their way into the city. But they seemed few in number.

"Where are the rest of them?" he wondered.

Within an hour Nimrod saw that a section of the defensive wall had been removed by his men, and a ramp had been built up leading over the ditch, which now belched black odorous clouds of smoke.

At Nimrod's command the trumpets sounded and the lancers

and charioteers rumbled into the city.

The charred, smoking bodies of Nimrod's foot soldiers could be seen littering the field outside the city. From his command post, Nimrod could not hear the groans of his wounded and dying men.

Fires now began to flare up all around Eshnunna, and the cries of women and children could be heard as their hiding places were discovered and they were dragged by the hair into the streets and put to the sword.

The king licked his lips and stared at the massacre taking place below him. He clenched his teeth in nervous excitement. "This is the fate of every worthless eater who refuses to submit to me and worship me," he murmured out loud.

Rising up to his full height he looked into the skies above him. "There is no God in the heavens. *I am God!*" he raged.

At that moment a ragtag band of fighters from Eshnunna swarmed over the king's hilltop command post, brandishing weapons they had taken from fallen Babylonian soldiers. Seeing the hopeless situation of their homes and families, these men banded together on a suicide mission to find the king and slay him. With the king's entourage focused on the battle, the raggedy group of men sneaking up the other side of the hill arrived unnoticed.

The only soldiers with Nimrod at that moment were messengers and banner bearers. Their attackers were not trained warriors, but they were inflamed with grief and a lust for revenge. They assailed the king's men on the hilltop with a savagery driven by desperation and the knowledge that this was their day to die.

Nimrod drew his sword and flew into his attackers, slashing wildly. A peasant of Eshnunna screamed in pain as a blow from the king severed his sword arm at the elbow. The man fell to his knees in agony. His agony did not last long for Nimrod's next blow expertly decapitated the man where he knelt.

Flush with bloodlust and adrenaline, Nimrod stopped and stared at the man he had just killed and began to howl with insane laughter. When he opened his eyes again he was staring into the face of another man of Eshnunna who held a sword at the king's throat.

From Nimrod's perspective everything around him was now moving in slow motion. He noticed that the man was skinny and rather smallish, barefoot and wearing a peasant's robe. His turban had fallen off and his long black hair hung in his face, which was streaked with blood, dirt, and sweat.

But what was this?

There was no look of savage conquest or revenge on the man's face. He was sad, grief-stricken. Tears rolled down his face. He didn't want to be doing this. With an animal scream the man pushed the sword through Nimrod's neck with all his strength.

Nimrod the Rebel stumbled backward and tripped over a rock at the edge of the cliff. Without a sound he went over and disappeared. His body crashed onto the sharp rocks far below.

Eshnunna, too, was dying.

CHAPTER TWENTY-THREE

Semiramis' Descent to the Underworld

An exhausted messenger lay prostrate on the floor of the queen's chamber. Semiramis stared at him, her heart pounding. This could not be good news.

"What is it, messenger? Speak!" she hissed through clenched teeth.

"O' Queen, Baalti, my Lady! Eshnunna is defeated, but the king has fallen in battle! The men are bringing his body back even now!"

Semiramis swallowed hard. Gasping for breath, she uttered one word, devoid of emotion.

"Leave."

The messenger scuttled on his hands and knees halfway across the queen's chamber toward the door then suddenly bolted upright to his feet and completed his exit, closing the door softly.

Her mind numb, the queen walked over to a bronze gong, and grasping the hammer, sent a crashing sound reverberating through the palace, causing every servant's head to jerk suddenly in her direction.

The sound of running footsteps in the hallway was followed by a knock at the door and the appearance of Itti-balatu, the palace administrator.

He folded his hands in front of his face, bowed at the waist, and said "Yes, Baalti, how may I serve my queen?"

"The king is dead," she announced abruptly.

"What!" the administrator gasped, raising his bald head and staring at the queen. "It can't be!"

The queen breathed deep, her eyes narrowed, and she glared condescendingly at Itti-balatu.

"It not only *can* be, it *is!* You incompetent fool! Your loyalty has always been questionable! You now have a chance to redeem yourself and perhaps save your life. The announcement is to be made publicly that the king has given his life fighting against the evil ones, the forces of the goddess Tiamat, who cause chaos and dissension. The king has given his life as a sacrifice for the good of the people!"

She continued, mesmerized, staring straight ahead. "Tiamat's forces of chaos are defeated because of the king's sacrifice. The priests are to be given his body when it arrives. They will know what to do. The people of Babylon will then observe a period of fasting and mourning to last forty days, one day for each year of the king's life."

Semiramis now approached the administrator, whom she towered over, and riveted him with her blazing eyes.

"I think it appropriate that the people demonstrate their willingness to suffer in some measure during the forty days. Don't you agree, Itti-balatu?"

Before he could respond, the queen was answering her own question.

"A little self-inflicted suffering, whips, knotted cords, knives, along with fasting and weeping. It is to be done publicly! Anyone who refuses is a traitor! Our king, Nimrod, shed his blood for them. The least they can do in appreciation is to shed a little of their own blood, in gratitude for his sacrifice!"

Her body stiffened and her eyes grew wide as a sudden ecstasy filled her. "It's the least they can do for a *god*, their *savior!*"

The administrator shrank away from the queen, and bowing profusely, said, "Yes, Baalti, of course. My lady is most wise. It will be done as you have said." He backed out of the room, still bowing up and down.

Alone now, Semiramis stood perplexed as reality began to sink in. "My husband is dead" she said out loud, as though needing to reinforce the fact to herself. "I have no son to take my husband's place as king. How will our work continue?"

"What will become of *me?*"

"I must seek the spirit masters now!" she cried.

She ran breathlessly down the hall to her private worship chamber, stopped at the threshold and peered inside.

Seeing the idol of Marduk leering back at her, she ran to him and fell at his feet. Fumes rising from the incense bowl next to the idol made her feel like her head was spinning. It was not incense smoldering in the dish. Whatever it was, it was having an immediate effect on her.

Raising her hands beseechingly she cried, "O' Marduk, lord of the gods, if ever I needed you it's now! Help me!"

Semiramis swooned as the idol's face slowly began to sparkle. Everything else in the room became as black as pitch. Then a ray of white light burst from Marduk's image, filling the room with a brilliance that made Semiramis instinctively raise her hands to shield her face. Peering through her fingers she saw space itself open like a rip in a garment. The rift widened until it engulfed her, and she found herself in the presence of two fierce beings of light.

She had made contact with the spirit guides many times, but as always she was almost overcome with a combination of fearful excitement and rushing adrenaline.

The ascended master she knew as Marduk, spoke. "Stand, Semiramis."

She stood with her hands clasped under her chin, wide-eyed and trembling.

"I knew you would help me, master!" she gushed.

"We are aware of your circumstances daughter." Marduk said. "We are here to assist you in your time of need. The one you see here beside me is called Ishtar."

Semiramis gazed at the being, who appeared radiant and terrible. "But we worship you as a *goddess*, a female" she said.

A crooked smile broke out on Ishtar's face. "We have no gender," he replied. "We are neither male nor female; we are spirit. We sometimes assume male or female attributes or tendencies in order to make ourselves more accessible and approachable to humans."

Marduk and Ishtar turned and looked at each other knowingly, like two adults who have just explained something elementary to a small child.

Marduk spoke again. "Your husband, the king, did indeed give his life as a sacrifice for the people. We channeled that thought to you. However, he has passed into the spirit realm now, and it is time to take you to the next level in your own spiritual evolution. Your initiation is incomplete. Do you have the will to complete it?"

"I do," Semiramis replied, without hesitating.

"We thought so," responded Marduk. "Ishtar will accompany

you on the journey you must take."

As an afterthought he said, "You will be reunited with your husband again, but not in a way you could possibly anticipate. Ishtar will tell you more at the proper time."

Semiramis nodded, speechless.

"Are you ready?" Ishtar asked sternly. He extended what appeared to be a hand to Semiramis.

"I am," came the reply, as she reached out and made contact with the leering spirit.

The surface under their feet opened up and Semiramis had the sickening sensation of falling over backward as she plummeted downward at breakneck speed. After falling for a horrifyingly indeterminate time she seemed to hit solid ground, experiencing a shock of sorts but no physical harm.

She stood up gasping, quaking with fright, and looked around. Why was it so cold? She was in what appeared to be an underground tunnel about ten feet wide and ten feet in height. She could not detect a light source, but there was just enough light, gloomy and pale, to see her way before her. The ground, walls, and ceiling were dank and moist, dripping or oozing some foul greenish liquid.

Where was the spirit guide, Ishtar? She whirled around looking for him and shrieked when she came face to face with him. He/she/it was not beautiful but hideous and menacing. It raised what resembled an arm, and pointing down the stinking corridor, said "Go."

"But where are we? Are you going with me? What am I supposed to do?" she said, all in one breath.

"Go," he replied.

Semiramis gulped, and lifting her gown several inches at the waist, she began tiptoeing down the gloomy stinking corridor. As she moved along she peered back over her shoulder to see if Ishtar was coming with her. He seemed to be following, or floating, at a distance behind her. Whatever lay ahead was apparently something she had to experience on her own.

She walked along, scared and cold, for perhaps an hour when she saw an object in the distance. As the structure loomed in front of her, she saw that it was a massive wooden door. She tried to open it but it wouldn't budge, so she knocked. She waited, then knocked again. She stood back, panic-stricken, and wrapped her arms around her shivering body. 'What if nothing happens? What if I am stranded in this awful place, with nowhere to go and no one to help me?'

Suddenly there was a creaking sound. The door opened and a tall hideous being slowly moved across the threshold, glaring at her contemptuously. Semiramis' impression, as always, during her encounters with the spirit beings, was that the spirits somehow had a mannish appearance, yet without conveying any real gender attributes. Sometimes they seemed kind, or at least instructive. This one was threatening and exuded evil intent. He/she/it spoke.

The voice sounded like the grinding of a millstone, "You enter Cthul, the realm of Eresh-kigal, Mistress of the Underworld. None who enter here may leave. There is no way back from the road that leads to the dark abode of Eresh-kigal. For the dwellers herein there is no light and dust is their food."

At this, Semiramis' anger flared. If she was to be initiated, then she would pass the test, no matter what spirits obstructed her.

"Stand aside gatekeeper," she commanded, "or I will tear this door from its post. I will raise up the dead so they outnumber the living!"

The gatekeeper stared at her balefully, then replied, "Stop Lady, do not tear down the door. I will announce your presence to Eresh-kigal." He drifted backward across the threshold and closed the door.

Several minutes passed before he reappeared and said to Semiramis menacingly, "Enter Lady, that Cthul may rejoice over you!"

His words struck Semiramis with terror, but summoning all of her courage she attempted to step through the threshold. The gatekeeper raised his hand to stop her.

"I will take your tiara, the symbol of your earthly majesty," he declared. When she protested he answered, "We follow the rules of Eresh-kigal, Mistress of Cthul." Semiramis handed over her tiara. Taking it, he said "Follow me."

Semiramis tiptoed and tripped her way along behind the gatekeeper, unable to determine the passage of time. Did they walk for ten minutes or ten hours? At last they reached another door rising up in the misty gloom. When they approached it the gatekeeper opened it then turned to Semiramis and announced, "You will give me your earrings." She looked at him silently. "We must follow the decrees of Eresh-kigal, Lady of the Underworld," he stated again matter of factly.

"Yes, yes, the decrees of Eresh-kigal," replied Semiramis sarcastically. "I must play by her rules — her, or him, or it — whatever you are!" She removed her earrings and handed them over to the gatekeeper.

They trudged on. Or she did rather, for the gatekeeper had no discernible legs or feet. He just silently floated along behind her.

After another wordless hike of unknown length, the two neared a third door in the dank underworld corridor. At this threshold the gatekeeper demanded her necklaces. Semiramis decided not to resist anymore.

They proceeded to a fourth door where the gatekeeper demanded that she hand over the gold-wired mesh that adorned her chest. At the fifth door he demanded the gold chain around her waist. At the sixth door she handed over the bracelets and anklets on her arms and feet.

At the seventh door Semiramis glared at the gatekeeper and said through clenched teeth, "All I have left is my gown. I suppose you want that too, you lecherous goon!" The gatekeeper extended what seemed to be an arm and said nothing. She removed her gown and undergarment, handed them to the gatekeeper, and stood naked and shivering.

"This is the last door," he said. "You now enter the presence of Eresh-kigal, Mistress of Cthul."

Semiramis tiptoed across the threshold and into a dark cavern. Her flesh crawled and she groaned with dreadful expectancy. Even so, she was not prepared for what happened next.

A bloodcurdling scream made Semiramis' heart stop, as a terrifying creature appeared in front of her, seated on what looked like a throne fashioned from a boulder.

Eresh-kigal.

Semiramis could not bring herself to look directly at this horrible monster. The thing called Eresh-kigal was a ghastly spirit with an eyeless face that seemed to be dripping like a melting candle. Her/his/its mid-section looked like molten metal, and its arms and legs like fire.

The Mistress of Cthul screeched at Semiramis, "I know why

you are here, you wretched jar of clay! You imagine yourself worthy of becoming one of *us*! You, a *goddess!* Uuurraaaghh!" Eresh-kigal made a nauseating vomiting sound that echoed off the walls of the cavern and stunned the queens' eardrums.

Reeling, Semiramis could only stare in shocked silence as Eresh-kigal continued her/his/its tirade. Summoning her chamberlain, Eresh-kigal screamed, "Namtar, lock her up! Unleash against her, who is to be hereafter called Ishtar, the sixty miseries!"

"Me... Ishtar?" said Semiramis.

Eresh-kigal continued ranting, "Misery of the eyes, misery of the sides, misery of the feet, misery of the head — against every part of her, against her whole body!"

Semiramis was instantly wracked with unimaginable pain. Her screams choked in her throat so that no sound emerged. As she looked down at herself in horror, a repulsive greenish skin disease began spreading from her torso down her arms and legs. Her fingers turned into bony claws and her ribs stood out like those of a skeleton.

As she doubled over in wrenching pain, another horrid spirit, Namtar, emerged. He immediately locked a chain on her wrist and jerked her along like a dog on a leash toward a black cave.

Unbeknownst to Eresh-kigal, another fallen spirit, Asushun-amir, had witnessed the scene and was now leaving to report to his superiors.

Appearing before Chulgomet, Asushun-amir related Semiramis' treatment at the hands of Eresh-kigal. "It goes badly Lord Chulgomet! The woman Semiramis will surely die if her abuse does not end."

Chulgomet grimaced, "Eresh-kigal exceeds his authority!

Return to him at once, Asushun-amir, and tell him this: 'The woman must surely live, for her work is not yet completed. She must become Ishtar. She will be worshipped as a goddess by many different names by all the tribes and nations of Earth! For by this false worship much of humanity will be led away from God and into our congregation!

"Tell Eresh-kigal" he continued, "that our master has decreed that Semiramis, as Ishtar, will be known to the peoples of Earth as:

> Ashtoreth, Astarte, Tsing-moo,
> Cybele, Isis, Danu, Ixchel,
> Disa, Nutria, Ceridwen, Venus,
> Juno, Rhea, Aphrodite, Nanna,
> Bridgid, Diana, Devaki, Imana,
> Baiame, Malina, Ptehehin-cala-sanwin,
> Awonawilona, Tse Na'ashji-ee
> Damballa, Artvahist-Indar, Hinay-
> nui-tepo, Chasca, Mary, Al-Lat,
> Omeciuatl, Teteo-inan, Xochiquetzal,
> Mahatala, Izanami, Gaia, Frigga,
> Kaira-Kan, Kwan Yin, Hertha...
> and by many, many other names!"

"Go now, Asushun-amir!" ordered Chulgomet. "Return to Eresh-kigal and warn him that the woman, Semiramis, must live!"

"Exceeding my authority?" seethed Eresh-kigal. "My authority comes from Lucifer himself!"

"Lord Eresh-kigal," responded Asushun-amir calmly, "as it concerns the woman Semiramis, the line of authority comes from the Lord Lucifer through Chulgomet. This is very clear. The woman must live so that Lord Ishtar may propagate his worship through her to all the Earth. We understand, do we not, Lord Eresh-kigal, that the worship of beings such as ourselves and Ishtar is in fact the worship of our master Lucifer! We do not own the glory given to us. It is passed on to the one who directs our struggle against the Creator, El Shaddai."

After a long silence Eresh-kigal screeched, "Namtar, bring the woman here!"

Namtar emerged from the cave dragging an unconscious Semiramis behind him. In the presence of Eresh-kigal and Asushun-amir, Namtar raised Semiramis to her feet and held her there until the disease left her. Her eyes finally opened and her breath returned.

"Get her out of here!" ranted Eresh-kigal.

Namtar led the wobbling, barely conscious Semiramis to the threshold of the door that entered Cthul, Eresh-kigal's domain, and turned her over to the gatekeeper who stood waiting. Noting her weakened condition the gatekeeper wrapped Semiramis' gown around her and fastened it.

The trip back through the remaining six doorways seemed endless to Semiramis. She trudged along, always at the point of exhaustion, until they reached another door, whereupon the gatekeeper would return to her the personal article of clothing or adornment that was taken from her earlier.

Stepping over the threshold of the final door the queen took her tiara from the gatekeeper, who immediately vanished. She turned her back to the door as it slammed shut, startling her. She placed the tiara on her head.

Instantly Ishtar appeared. This time he seemed kind and

supportive but Semiramis' instincts told her to be wary. As they returned through the long dark corridor Ishtar gave continuous instruction to the queen concerning the role she was now to play in the affairs of humanity.

When they arrived at the spot in the corridor where Semiramis had originally fallen, Ishtar turned her to face him. With his eyes blazing he gave her his last command, then merged into her and possessed her.

Back in her palace Semiramis stepped from her private worship chamber and hurried down the hallway. Upon reaching her room she immediately strode to the brass gong and sent a loud crash through the palace. When the palace administrator arrived, panting, she turned to him and said, "Summon the nobles, the soldiers, and all the people of Babylon. The day after tomorrow, at noon, I will speak to them in the courtyard of the Sacred Precinct."

When the time arrived, many thousands of people crammed the Sacred Precinct to hear the words of the widow of King Nimrod.

"Will Semiramis rule in Nimrod's place?" wondered all the people.

A golden throne was placed at the top of the massive stairway leading up to the temple of Marduk. Clouds of smoke billowed as incense was poured into the giant bronze burners on either side of the throne.

At last the queen appeared, arrayed as a goddess in a dazzling white gown, adorned with gold jewelry and a glittering crown.

Standing in front of the throne she began her announcement, as attendants relayed her words throughout the crowd.

"My husband, your king, has given himself as a sacrifice for the people, that they may be forgiven of their sins and may take their place one day with the gods. Your king has become the sun god, worthy of all praise and worship! He intercedes on your behalf with the gods who rule over you. And the tower behind you, Etemenanki, which rises to the sky, is hereby dedicated to him! The temple on top of it — Dur Anki, the Bond of Heaven and Earth — will be the place where the great realm of the spirit lords meets the realm of mankind."

"And I... I have become Ishtar, the Queen of Heaven!"

CHAPTER TWENTY-FOUR

Etemen-anki, the Tower of Babel

"**R**eza!" boomed the young man's father, Zakir.

Zakir, the brick-maker, walked out into the brickyard and looked around with his hands on his hips. Scanning the area, he saw his employees scurrying about their tasks. New orders were coming in every day as the public works projects begun by Nimrod continued under the administration of his queen, Semiramis, who was now known officially as the goddess Ishtar.

"Reza, where are you?" he yelled.

No answer.°

Approaching a foreman, Zakir queried, "Nerari, have you seen my son? It's time for us to go home for our mid-day meal."

Nerari looked at his employer with a mischievous grin. But before he could speak, Zakir laughed out loud. "Oh, let me guess! He's gotten a head-start on me," he said, chuckling. "I think I know where to find him!"

Nerari nodded his head and laughed. "Master Reza's mind is not in his work these days! I am happy for him. When will the marriage take place Master Zakir?"

"Very soon, I believe, Nerari. And you and your wife will certainly be there, as our honored guests!"

Nerari bowed and held his folded hands to his forehead. "My

lord Zakir is gracious to his servant Nerari!" he replied humbly.

"You're a good man, Nerari!" Zakir said, and turned to make his way toward the marketplace, where he knew he would find Reza.

There was a bounce in Zakir's step as he strode through the crowded streets of Babylon that day. His prayers concerning his son had been answered. Reza had been shown the truth behind the new religion with its dark teachings and forbidden knowledge. That became evident when Zakir opened the door of his home several days ago and encountered his old friend Amel-labashi accompanied by a chastened and humbled Reza.

As Zakir walked along, he wondered to himself at the capacity of the human heart to break with pity and compassion while at the same time rejoicing with unspeakable joy. He and his wife, Ishabi, experienced these cascading emotions as they watched their son, Reza, fall to his knees sobbing and begging their forgiveness.

'It is one thing to see a little child cry; it is something altogether different to watch a child who has grown into manhood break down in a flood of tears and remorse,' thought Zakir.

The reconciliation that followed was blessed; and Reza's reconciliation with Vashti, the love of his life, was not only blessed but also incredibly sweet. It took some cajoling to get her to come to her kitchen table to meet with Reza and his father and mother. Once there, she was defensive and had few words to say. To protect her own heart she would not look at Reza and kept her head covering pulled close around her face, revealing only her eyes.

It was the calm reassuring intervention of Reza's mother, Ishabi, that finally alerted Vashti to the change of heart in her estranged love. When that moment occurred and Vashti turned and made eye contact with Reza, she choked back a sob and got up and ran to the garden in the courtyard of her family's home.

Reza found her kneeling beside the pool of water in the center of the garden. He knelt next to her and put his hand on her shoulder. She did not pull away, but turned her head and looked into his face. Her countenance spoke of a desire to believe and be restored to her love, but also of lingering doubt.

'This is too good to be true,' she thought. 'Can it be? Is he just saying these things? Oh God, El Shaddai, if you only speak to my heart one time, let it be now!'

The lovers' reunion was sweet.

Meanwhile the parents, soon to be in-laws, decided to take a long walk around the neighborhood to allow the young lovers time to be reconciled with each other. As they walked, the women discussed plans for the upcoming marriage while the men appraised the situation in Babylon.

As they rounded a street corner, the ominous pyramid tower, Etemen-anki, loomed into view. Vashti's father, Samsu-iluna, gazed at the foreboding structure in the distance then turned and looked at Zakir.

"That tower represents all that is wrong with the world," he shuddered. "El Shaddai will not allow it to stand."

Etemen-anki, the great brooding tower of Babylon, was nearing completion. All the people of Earth were of one basic language, with regional and tribal dialects, but everyone understood that the tower's name meant 'House of the Foundation of Heaven and Earth'. The reason for such a name, however, was beyond their comprehension.

On top of the tower, a temple had been raised to the sun god. The temple was called Dur Anki, which meant Bond of Heaven and Earth. It was intended to be the place where the powers of earth interacted with the powers in the spirit realm.

In this temple were quarters for the *mashmashu* priests, as well as for the *sa anga*, or high priest, and a separate chamber equipped with a large bed with a golden frame. Each night a woman was chosen to sleep on this bed to serve as a lover for the sun god. It was rumored though that the priests took advantage of this arrangement and took turns making late night visits to the chamber with the golden bed.

On the roof of Dur Anki an enormous golden disk, carved with the image of the sun god, had been hung between two stone pillars. This disk would reflect the sun god's brilliant glory for all the people to see.

The temple also had an inner room called the Holy of Holies, which was off limits to everyone but the high priest. In this chamber was a golden statue of the sun god with a halo. The halo represented the sun and was the symbol of its worship. Also in the Holy of Holies was a golden altar upon which was the fabled emerald Tablet of Destiny which described the movements, functions, and fates of the planetary gods. It also described a wandering rogue planet, and its deity, that visited the solar system periodically. The Tablet also detailed the exploits of the Nephilim, the mighty beings who were cast down from the heavens and taught secret knowledge to humans. It was death for anyone but the priests to look upon the sacred Tablet of Destiny.

In the Holy of Holies the priests would make contact with the ascended masters, the spirits who channeled information and teachings directly to their human representatives. New religious practices were thus formulated; practices that did not originate with the only true God, the Heavenly Father and Creator.

In hushed tones it was whispered among the people that grisly ceremonies had taken place in the temple Dur Anki involving the body of Nimrod. It was said that the *mashmashus* had been instructed by the spirit guides to *eat* the king's body. The practice was made part of the secret inner rituals of the mystery religion. The priests called the ceremony 'eating the god', and whoever participated would partake of the divine nature themselves.

By order of the *sa anga* and Queen Semiramis, small round barley cakes were being mass produced for the purpose of simulating the eating of the god ceremony. The *mashmashus* would murmur magical incantations over the cakes, supposedly transforming them into the actual body of the sun god. The cakes would then be eaten by worshippers. Curiously, the cakes were stamped with an image of Semiramis, as Ishtar, with twelve stars above her head and a crescent moon under her feet. The twelve stars represented the twelve principal gods of the Babylonian pantheon.

Most curious of all was the elaborate ceremony performed by the officiating priest leading up to the eating of the god. This complicated ritual, channeled to the priests by the ascended masters, also called spirit guides, began with the priest touching his forehead, then his chest, then one shoulder, then the other. This was done repeatedly as the priest turned to the worshippers and looked heavenward. The priest would then lean over and kiss the altar, strike his chest, kneel down, bow his head, stand, turn back to the altar, touch his forehead, chest, and shoulders again, pray silently, then loudly, and finally, take the basket with the round barley cakes and utter magical chants that transformed the bread into the god's body. Further enhancing this spectacle were the priests' colorful robes and incense, music, bells, candles, and singing.

The people were awed.

But not all of them.

CHAPTER TWENTY-FIVE

The Godly Remnant

All evening shadowy figures had been making their way down Nebu Street, just behind the Temple of Marduk in the Sacred Precinct of Babylon. Pausing at a certain doorway, the figures would glance furtively up and down the street then quickly slip into the home of Amel-labashi, leader of the Dakuri tribe and the recognized spokesman for the remaining followers of God, El Shaddai.

Assembled in the open-air courtyard of Amel-labashi's home for the clandestine meeting were the elders and chieftains of tribes and clans who remained loyal to the one true God. These godly men and women had witnessed the decline of humanity into violence, spirit worship, and immorality, and could not stand by passively any longer. They understood that to do nothing would eventually be disastrous for themselves and their families.

Their distress and concern were greatly intensified by Queen Semiramis' public announcement that she had been impregnated by a *sunbeam* issuing from the sun god directly into her body. The sun god, declared the queen and supported by the priests, was none other than her deceased husband Nimrod, reincarnated as a god!

Finally, adding shock upon shock, she said that the child she was carrying *was* Nimrod, her husband/child, to be reborn as the savior of the people!

The time for action had come.

Under a moonless summer sky, Amel-labashi stood, his head uncovered, and addressed the people. Their solemn faces were lit only by flickering oil lamps on the columns surrounding the courtyard.

"My friends, we gather tonight under the loving gaze of our God and Father, the one we know as El Shaddai, the almighty God, who has given us everything we need to live godly lives in him. May he be praised forever! You have been summoned here tonight to discuss matters of the utmost importance that affect every one of us and our children as well."

Having the attention of his audience, he continued. "Now, you all know how our ancestors were destroyed in the Great Flood for turning their backs on God and following the teachings of demons, calling them gods, and giving in to the lusts of their own flesh. My friends, do not be deceived, God is not mocked! A man reaps what he sows. If we sow to the flesh we will reap destruction, but if we sow to the spirit of God we will reap eternal life."

All heads nodded in agreement.

"The lesson of the Flood has not been learned by the rest of the people" Amel said sadly. "They are repeating the errors our ancestors made. God is holy, and he desires a holy people. He cannot tolerate sin and rebellion and remain true to his own nature, which is pure and righteous. He is just. In fact, he *is* justice. Sin brings judgment. Only fools are unaware of this!

"Now," Amel continued, "our friend, Nadin-shah, chief of the Yamutbal tribe, has a word for us."

A robust, middle-aged man stood and cleared his throat.

"Greetings, and peace to you my friends." Nadin-shah smiled, then became deadly serious.

"You are no strangers to what has occurred in our midst. Nimrod and Semiramis have introduced new gods to us, who are not gods at all, but fallen spirits. But they would have us acknowledge them as gods! They have filled our city and all the other towns and villages with idols of these rebel spirits and have commanded the people to worship them.

"They have instituted a priesthood for this corrupt religion and they tax the people to support it. This religion of Marduk, Ishtar, and the other spirits, is leaving its stain on every aspect of our lives. Our children cannot marry unless the priests officiate and record it. When we borrow money for business or buy property we must make our vows of repayment to ... which god is it now, Enlil, Nergal, some other? No matter. It is not the true God and Creator of everything."

"It is the fashion now to take the name of one of these false gods as part of our own names. Some from our own tribes have done this." Nadin-shah lamented.

At this, a number of heads in the crowd drooped in shame.

Nadin-shah continued, "Nimrod declared himself Pontifex Maximus, the Supreme Bridge-Keeper. By so doing, he declared himself God, with power over the eternal destiny of souls. This title has also been claimed by the high priest of the false religion who claims for himself powers and authority that he does not have, nor ever will. His successors will, no doubt, do likewise.

"Queen Semiramis claims that Nimrod, a man, and a dead one at that, is the sun god. And the priests, God help us, are slithering, like the serpents they are, into every aspect of our lives, and charging us a fee for every service! We can't even bury our dead without having to pay the priests to chant their prayers and wave their incense burners over the bodies of our loved ones! They make us and our children bow down before idols and relics as though those things were holy in and of themselves!"

The people in Amel-labashi's courtyard murmured their displeasure while several stood and proclaimed their loyalty to El Shaddai. A number of women began to softly wail, swaying from side to side as they sat on the ground weeping.

A woman named Shalti stood and spoke out boldly. "My son, Mukeen, attended the writing-school, the *Eduba*. My husband and I sent him there to learn writing and numbers so he could help us manage our business. Well, the priests have taken over the schools and they require all students to pray to Marduk and Enlil each day and are recruiting our children to be initiated into their priesthood. We protested and took Mukeen out of the school, but the priests made us pay the fees for another student to replace him. The queen's soldiers came to our home to collect the money!"

A farmer named Shakusha stood and addressed the assembly. "I live in the countryside. There the priests have erected altars in every high place and hilltop they can find. They are making the people in the villages go up to the high places and pray to the false gods. Shakusha then lowered his head, ashamed. "The priests are encouraging the people to have orgies at the high places and they even send male and female temple prostitutes who charge a fee for their services."

A woman in the crowd cried out, "How can we teach our children to be pure when the priests teach immorality?"

The crowd murmured again.

Amel-labashi spoke. "The priests even say we must go to *them* and confess our sins. We have always spoken directly with El Shaddai. *He* hears our prayers. He is loving and forgiving. He is not deaf to his children."

The people began to shout their agreement, but Amel-labashi immediately held up his hands to quiet them.

"Remember, we are meeting illegally!" he cautioned them. "What we are doing now is treason to the queen and the priests."

Zakir, the brick-maker said, "What does Abu-eshu say? Where is father Abu? What does the elder of elders say about all this?"

A commotion rippled through the crowd.

"Where is Abu-eshu?"

All eyes landed on an old fellow who struggled to his feet with the help of two of his grandsons. His tiny wife, Gula, took her place beside him, holding his arm. Abu was the chief elder of the Amurru tribe and was the oldest man anyone knew about.

There was absolute silence as the gnarled, white-headed old man leaned on a staff and began to speak. The flickering lamplight made him look even more ancient than he was.

In a rising voice, Abu-eshu spoke to the people. "After the Flood, our ancestors lived in the Zagros mountains to the east while the earth dried out. When the earth was again dry so that men could walk on it they wandered down from the mountains onto the plain of Shinar and planted fields and founded cities. They dug canals and drained the marshes. The teachings of Father Noah concerning the one true God, the one we know as El Shaddai, were passed on faithfully from generation to generation."

A bemused look passed over Abu's weathered face. "We know the truth about God, don't we, my friends?" he said, looking around with a toothless grin. "He is one, not many. He is a personality, not an idea or a force. He is not nature. He *created* nature. He is a good and loving father, not a wicked and spiteful tyrant. He gives us a free will and a conscience to enable us to freely choose what is good and to live according to his perfect will. When we sin and break his laws he desires only that we repent and be restored to him again. For this reason he makes a way of atonement, forgiveness, and reconciliation. He does not leave us helpless or abandoned as orphans.

"He wants his children to freely love him. That is why he made us in his spiritual image. That is why, when we die in his grace, he takes the departed soul to be with him. And we know, my friends," he said, filled with the Spirit of God and almost hopping up and down with joy, "that some day our Father will renew the Earth and will give us glorified bodies and a kingdom!"

The people replied as one, "Amen, may it be so!"

"So then," Abu-eshu continued, looking around the courtyard, "where are the men and women among you who remain loyal to our Father in heaven? I am not calling for war. Would our God have us become violent, like the soldiers of Babylon? No! Our God is saying 'Come out of Babylon, my people! Do not be like her! Come out and be a people set apart for myself, and I will be your God!'"

Abu-esha's voice suddenly became stern and unnaturally amplified. "Prepare to leave!" he cried out. "God's fearful judgment will soon fall on this city and its inhabitants!"

Abu-esha slowly sat down, fatigued. His wife lovingly tended to him.

Amel-labashi stood again and announced, "What tribes are represented here?"

The tribal names were announced: "Yakin, Dakuri, Amukani,

Eriba, Amurru, Yamutbal, Sutu, Tidnum, Rabbaya!"

Amel-labashi continued, nodding his head with his hands on his hips. "Very well, then. The chiefs and elders of the tribes will meet here again in three days, by night. We will discuss plans for the departure and resettlement of our people. Are we in agreement?"

The response was positive and unanimous.

In the vortex whirling above Babylon a report was being delivered. Chulgomet addressed the assembly. "The High Council has met and has reached a decision. The Lord Lucifer concurs with us. You have all been instructed, Colleagues — 'as above, so below'. What originates in the heavenly realm is manifested on earth in the physical realm. And so it is. If the Creator's plan is to provide a savior born to a woman then we will provide one first! A forgery! A counterfeit! And this deception will go out into all the world to lead the nations astray, for when the true savior/redeemer is born, he will have been preceded by many false savior/redeemers."

A great roar of approval erupted within the vortex.

But the rebellious spirits' celebration would not have been as exuberant if they had known that the hammer of God's judgment was about to fall.

-→ CHAPTER TWENTY-SIX ⟵-

The Hammer of Judgment

Months passed, and the people of Babylon were in a state of near hysteria as the day approached for the birth of Semiramis' child. The emotions ran the spectrum of high excitement for the populace in general, to that of intense dread for those who remained loyal to God. To those godly men and women, the birth of this child, whether male or female, was a chilling portent of calamity. All the more so since their tribal leaders, men like Amel-labashi, Nadin-shah, and even old Abu-eshu, had been recently reported to the authorities and were arrested and imprisoned for treason and impiety against the gods.

Semiramis became withdrawn and morose in the latter stages of her pregnancy. She spent her days in her private worship chamber communing with Marduk and Ishtar. The only person admitted into her personal chambers was the high priest, the *sa anga*. Her hatred of El Shaddai, the God of Creation, and his followers, became obsessive, and in her mounting paranoia she declared the faith in God the Creator to be illegal and punishable by imprisonment, torture, and confiscation of land and property.

The people were required to assemble weekly in the Sacred Precinct for the public worship of Nimrod, as the sun god. As the sun reflected off the great golden disk on top of the tower Etemen-anki, the people would bow low, their faces to the ground, and offer their worship to the sun god.

The believers in the true God did their best to avoid these assemblies, but risked arrest if discovered. They discreetly continued their plans to leave the city, building wagons and stockpiling provisions. The reason given for these activities was a desire to open up new farmlands and orchards in the distant countryside, which was actually true. However, if it became known that their motive was to escape the moral pollution of Babylon and its false religion, they would not only be prevented, they would face prison, or worse.

The birth of the child, a boy, occurred in the middle of the night, on the first day of the month called Tebit. The queen's astrologers murmured amongst themselves that this was a bad sign, for Tebit was an unlucky month, in which ghosts and demons were prone to walk amongst humans and cause mischief. However, this unfortunate timing was overruled by an unusual and auspicious celestial event.

The *sa anga* and the astrologers were carefully watching the skies that night from the top of Etemen-anki and were delighted to observe that a great luminous halo formed around the moon. This in itself was a sign of good fortune. As the evening wore on and Semiramis' labor became intense, the astrologers watched, elated, as Ishtar's planet, Venus, rose...inside the halo surrounding the moon! It was a great, momentous omen — the two brightest lights in the night sky together within a celestial halo! Ishtar and the moon god, Sin, were cohabiting; the child would be blessed!

The *sa anga* was allowed into the birthing area in the queen's chambers to deliver the news. Having just received her newborn child from the midwives, Semiramis, drenched in sweat, looked up at the *sa anga* and declared proudly, "My husband is reborn!"

The high priest stared at her speechless.

The news of the child's birth spread throughout Babylon like wildfire the next day. Mounted messengers took the news to all the towns and villages. Along with this news came a command; on the first day of the third month following the boy's birth, all the people were to assemble in the Sacred Precinct in Babylon. Every person's presence was required. No exceptions.

When that day arrived it witnessed the largest gathering of people the world had ever seen. All of humanity was assembled in Babylon to see the child of Semiramis presented and named. The city was literally overflowing with people. Every street and alley was filled, every rooftop packed with the curious. Everyone who could get close to the Sacred Precinct focused their attention on the platform at the top of the stairs leading up to the Temple of Marduk, opposite the tower Etemen-anki.

The crowd's excitement rose to fever pitch as men appeared at the top of the stairs carrying a golden throne on poles. Perched on the throne was the queen, dressed in a purple robe, hemmed in gold. The men set the throne down facing the crowd and removed the poles.

Great clouds of smoke rose up as priests poured sacks of incense into bronze burners set up on either side of the throne. The *sa anga* approached the queen and bowed to the ground, then rose and faced the crowd, holding up his hands for silence. Then he began to lead the people in worship.

"Hail, Lady of Ladies, Goddess of Goddesses,
Ishtar, Queen of the earth, leader of all people!
You are the light of the world, you are the light of
heaven. Supreme is your might, O Lady, exalted
are you above the gods! You render judgment,
and your decisions are righteous!

The laws of heaven and earth are subject to you,
the laws of the temples and the shrines, the laws
of the private home and the secret chamber!

Where is the place where you are not known, and
where is the place where your commandments
are not known?

At your name the earth and the heavens shake,
and the gods tremble! You look upon the
oppressed, and to the downtrodden you bring
justice every day!

Do not tarry O' Queen of Heaven and Earth.
Do not tarry, O' Shepherdess of men,
Lady of Hosts, Lady of Battles.

Glorious one whom all the spirits of heaven fear,
who subdues all angry gods, mighty above all
rulers, who holds the reins of man and gods!
Opener of the wombs of all women, great is your
light!

Shining light of heaven, light of the world,
enlightener of all the places where people dwell,
who gathers together the hosts of the tribes!

Goddess of men, Divinity of women, your counsel
passes understanding!

Where you cast your gaze, the dead come to life,
and the sick rise and walk. The mind of the diseased
is healed when it looks upon your face!

Command, O' Lady, and at your command the angry
gods will turn back!

Ishtar is great! Ishtar is Queen! Our Lady is exalted!
There is none like her in heaven or earth!

Praise Ishtar!"

The multitudes shouted as one, "Praise Ishtar!"

In the vortex Chulgomet convened a small gathering of high-
level spirit lords.

"Beautiful!" he exulted. "Our master's plan is working! Ishtar,
have you channeled the teaching concerning the fire sacrifice to
the queen?"

The spirit Ishtar replied, "Yes Lord Chulgomet."

Chulgomet turned to the other spirit authorities present.
"Molech," he said to one of them, "you have your instructions. You
and your cohorts will instruct the humans to sacrifice their children
to yourselves and to our master Lucifer in fire. Burnt sacrifices!
Severe punishments are to be inflicted by human authorities on
those parents who refuse to comply. Then their children will be
taken from them and sacrificed anyway."

Chulgomet continued. "We have them worshipping Nimrod as the sun god. Notice how easily we displace the Creator as the humans' objects of worship! They wouldn't worship Nimrod if they knew his actual whereabouts, would they my lords? For Nimrod, that is his soul, the part of him that lives after his physical death, lies at rest awaiting judgment, for he died as a disobedient rebel against God."

The spirit called Baal-Zebub, suddenly filled with dread, murmured to himself, "If such is the fate of these rebellious jars of clay, what is to become of *us,* who beheld the glory of God and served in his presence with honor and authority?"

Standing before all the people, the queen, Semiramis, presented herself as the goddess Ishtar. Announcers relayed her words throughout the crowds.

"I am Ishtar, the Queen of Heaven!" she cried.

"Praise Ishtar, Queen of Heaven!" roared the crowd.

She continued, "Your king, Nimrod, who gave his life as a blood sacrifice for your sins, went to take his place as the sun god. Later, as you have already heard, he impregnated me with his divine sunbeam, and the child — no, the *god,* within me, was Nimrod himself! He has now been born, my subjects. My husband/child has been born! He is the savior and the redeemer of mankind. His new name is Tammuz, the one who purifies by fire! For the sins of the people will be purged by fire!"

At this prompting, the *sa anga* brought forward the naked baby boy and handed him to the queen. At the same moment the vortex over the tower Etemen-anki began to churn with intense energy as hoards of spirits prepared to depart for their assignments.

The queen raised the child and presented him to the worshipping masses.

"Behold, your god and savior!"

As the people bowed and praised their new god and goddess, the *sa anga* declared, "The sculptors and artisans of Earth are hereby ordered by our goddess Ishtar to begin the manufacture of statues, idols, carvings, paintings, and all manner of art and craft to represent our goddess, the Queen of Heaven, with her holy child. These creations will be objects of adoration and worship and remembrance of the goddess and her husband/child in all places, at all times!"

The vortex became electrified as Chulgomet gave orders to the hierarchy of spirits. "Colleagues, you are to exert your influence in every area of human activity: in their worship, in male/female relations, in parent/child relations, in their work, in their rest, in wealth, in poverty, in eating, in sleeping, in waking, in walking, in talking, in their sexuality, in malice, in lying, in the exploitation of the weak and the poor, in abuses, in bloodshed, in the courts, with governing authorities, in the arts and crafts, in knowledge, in occultic secrets, in things done under cover of night and in closed rooms, in murders, wars, destruction and turmoil, in diseases, in the lust for power and control, in the exploitation and abuse of the earth's resources. Colleagues, your work is before you!"

Chulgomet, insane with his own power and corruption, continued raving, "You have your tasks. You are assigned to tribes, clans, and nations. You will move with them wherever they go. You will do whatever is required to lead them away from the Creator. You are to steal, kill and destroy their lives and their hopes, by any means necessary!

"Go forth you Lords, Dignitaries, and Authorities, you and your captains and all the hordes who serve under you! Go!"

At Chulgomet's command the vortex began to empty itself like sand flowing from a broken hourglass. Innumerable spirits poured forth like a vast cloud of flitting bats from the bottom of the vortex.

Then, passing through the great golden sun disk on top of the tower Etemen-anki, the malignant cloud spread out over the area where humanity had gathered, casting a giant shadow, invisible to mortal eyes, over many square miles. The spirits were ready to move down and infiltrate their assigned people groups.

At that moment a deathly stillness gripped every soul and spirit as darkness, like a shadowy hand, moved across the face of the sun. All the people stood, open-mouthed and astonished, as an eerie brownish hue descended over land and sky, along with a tense silence.

The *sa anga* whirled around and stared desperately at an astrologer who shook his head in confusion, saying "Impossible, my lord *sa anga*, an eclipse will not occur until the 28th day of the month of Kislev!"

'Strange,' thought the *sa anga*, 'he's never spoken like that before. I couldn't understand him at all.'

The *sa anga* whirled back around to face the queen, who remained frozen, still holding her child aloft before the crowds.

"My Queen, Lady Ishtar, what is happening?" asked the distraught high priest.

The queen turned and stared at him with a puzzled look on her face. "What...did you just say, *sa anga*?" she said, slowly lowering the child to her lap.

The *sa anga* brought his face close to the queen's and repeated, "My Lady, Ishtar, what is happening?"

The queen recoiled in horror. "Are you mad?" she screeched. "I don't understand what you're saying! Why are you talking that way?"

Clutching her baby to her breast she stood and slowly backed away from the *sa anga*.

A panic was now taking hold of the masses of people below, as accents and dialects that previously were mutually understood suddenly became muddled to the point of incomprehension. People shouted louder and louder as they sought out someone, anyone, who could understand them and explain the bizarre things that were happening.

Groups began to form, like raindrops coalescing into puddles, as individuals clung to others who understood their speech. As it was, these gathering groups represented the tribes and clans, who now only understood the speech of those related to them through kinship and ethnicity.

Fear yielded to unrestrained hysteria as soldiers shouted orders at people who could not understand, then murderously attacked them for disobedience. The soldiers, unable to communicate with each other, turned their weapons upon one another, fearing treason.

Holy angels, loyal to the God of all Creation, entered the riot in large numbers, gathering protectively around those who remained faithful to their heavenly Father. Like doting shepherds, the holy angels led their charges away from dangerous situations to safe places where their tribesmen and kinfolk could be found. Once safe with their own people, a sense of peace prevailed, even excitement, as the awareness settled in that the time had come for their deliverance and separation from Babylon and all its ungodliness and immorality.

The word spread rapidly among the godly tribes — "the time has come. Gather your loved ones and belongings and proceed to your tribe's designated meeting place outside the city."

For some, an errand of mercy remained.

Reza, the brick-maker's son, and five other young men made their way through the chaotic streets of Babylon to the building housing the royal dungeons of the queen, determined to liberate the godly men imprisoned there. Armed with swords taken from dead soldiers in the streets, Reza and his band warily descended the steps into the dungeon where prisoners were held in filthy cells. Expecting a fight, they were amazed to find that the soldiers guarding the prisoners had apparently turned on one another in a bloody panic. Their bodies lay scattered on the floor. If anyone survived, they must have fled.

Wasting no time, the young rescuers began calling out the names of the men they were looking for. Finding them, they were immediately released from their cells. Old Abu-eshu praised God loudly as two young men helped him up the stairs to the street. Seeing the light of day he exclaimed, "Blessed am I indeed to live to see the deliverance of God's people!"

One of the young men helping Abu-eshu understood him perfectly. The other simply stared at him, unable to understand at all.

When Reza and his cohorts were several blocks away from the dungeon, the chieftain, Amel-labashi, drew them all aside into an alleyway and gave them an urgent briefing.

"The judgment of El Shaddai has come. We must go to our tribes and our kinfolk and leave Babylon, never to return," he said solemnly. Several of the men stared at him and shrugged their shoulders, unable to comprehend. Seeing their confusion, Amel-labashi spoke the names of the men's tribes and clans, then said "Go!" This they understood, and after embracing everyone in the group, each man turned and ran to find his people.

Reza now had but one thought — Vashti.

Taking his leave of the others, Reza ran toward his love's neighborhood. By now looting and destruction were rampant and people ran for their lives clutching the possessions they could carry. Distraught parents screamed helplessly for their missing children as fires began to spread from building to building. Bands of soldiers inflicted violence randomly on passersby. Reza avoided the soldiers, and being armed with a sword, he passed through the streets relatively unmolested.

He now turned down Vashti's street. He was aware that he was not experiencing the kind of crazed hysteria that gripped most of the people around him. However, the feeling of dread rose in him as he picked his way through the smoky, rubble-strewn neighborhood. Then he froze, horror-struck. Her home was ablaze.

From a distance he saw a thick cloud of dust billow into the street as the front wall of her family's home collapsed, its charred wooden beams no longer supporting it.

Leaping over the rubble into her home, Reza ran through the crackling inferno shouting, "Vashti! Vashti! Is anyone here?"

Overwhelmed by the flames and smoke, he was forced to retreat into the street. Had she gone to *his* home, looking for him? he wondered.

He turned and ran toward his own home. Several times he raised his sword against a threatening looter or to rescue a woman or children being attacked or abused.

Reza's heart raced as he ran down his own street. He spied his family's home and noted with relief that it was not burning. His relief soon turned to despair. After running through the house and checking every room, he realized that there was no one there. He knelt down in the front hallway exhausted and panting. 'Will I ever see Vashti alive again?' he moaned. 'And what about my parents and brothers and sisters? What has become of them?'

Then he remembered the instructions given by Amel-labashi concerning Reza and Vashti's tribe, the Amukani. In the event of an evacuation, the Amukani were to assemble on the plateau of Eridu, several miles to the northeast of Babylon. Perhaps his family, and Vashti's, had already left Babylon to join up with the rest of the tribe.

His hope rekindled, Reza stood and breathed deeply. Walking to the front door of his home, he gazed up and down the street in awe at the obvious panic and hysteria on the faces of the people he saw.

"No wonder," he thought. "They have no hope. They don't know God. They don't understand that he loves everyone who comes to him in faith, and he rejects no one, not even the lowliest slave."

Then a sobering truth came to Reza. 'They knew the truth about God but they turned away from him and followed spirits who were not even gods! They willingly chose to worship God's enemies instead of God himself!' Reza thought. Then a startling realization came to him.

"How close I came to making the same mistake!"

He shuddered and whispered a prayer of thanks.

'God's judgments are just,' he concluded.

Stepping from his home for the last time, Reza turned and started off with a loping stride toward the eastern city gate at the far end of Marduk Street.

Later, as he drew close to the eastern gate, he saw that he was not the only one trying to leave the city; there was a flood of humanity, shouting and cursing in a frightened panic, flowing through the streets toward the city gates. Reza realized that such hysteria was not normal. Something was causing this, driving the people in this way, turning on each other violently, without reason, mindlessly fleeing their homes and belongings.

Reza knew instinctively that this was God's judgment.

As he neared the city gate Reza was prepared to fight his way out but it became apparent that the handful of soldiers there could do nothing to stop such a huge, surging crowd. He became part of the river of humanity flowing out of the City of Babylon. Once past the city gate the rest of the crowd followed the road but Reza broke away and ran across open country toward Eridu plateau.

As Reza slowed to catch his breath, still a mile or so from the plateau, he could see that a crowd of people had indeed gathered there, and there were others trekking in from many directions. His hope rose in him and he began to run again.

As Reza passed others of his tribe he noticed that there was none of the panic or hysteria in them that gripped the rest of the Babylonians. He passed an elderly couple who clung to each other supportively as they slowly shuffled along. Reza had compassion on them and stopped to encourage them. He was surprised to see them look up at him and smile serenely.

The old man said, "El Shaddai is delivering his people from evil. We are free to begin a new life!" His wife nodded in agreement.

Reza continued on, straining his eyes ahead in the gloom for some sign of his love. As he scanned the area at the base of the plateau, something caught his attention. Everyone else was moving in the same direction as Reza, toward the plateau. But there was one lone figure moving away from the plateau toward him. It was a female wearing a blue robe and head covering.

Reza stood still, not breathing, unwilling to let himself believe what he desperately wanted to believe.

As the young woman got closer her face came into focus.

"Reza!" she cried, now running.

"Ohh..." Reza exhaled, as indescribable joy welled up within him. "Vashti!" he moaned to himself as he began to run toward her.

"Reza!" she screamed again. As they neared each other Vashti leaped in the air wrapping her arms and legs around Reza, who clutched her tightly. Setting her gently on the ground, they gazed, trembling, into each other's eyes, then embraced.

As they walked toward the plateau Vashti assured Reza that his family, and hers, were alright. Hand in hand, they exchanged the stories of their escape from Babylon.

It was a relieved reunion atop Eridu plateau as Reza's grateful family surrounded him and hugged him. His father, Zakir, grabbed him by the shoulders and said, "We didn't know if you were alive or dead, son!"

His mother, Ishabi, nodded tearfully and added, "We were afraid we had lost you Reza, but El Shaddai has blessed us!"

Then, sensing that something else was about to happen, Reza took Vashti by the hand and led her to the edge of the plateau. In the distance was the city of Babylon with black smoke rising from every quarter. Most prominent of all was the great sinister tower,

Etemen-anki — the tower of Babylon — still rising proudly in the midst of the city.

As they stood with their arms around each other, gazing at the incredible sight, Reza and Vashti felt the ground rumbling under their feet. Stepping away from the edge of the plateau, they stared, astonished, as the tower Etemen-anki trembled and shook, then cracked vertically from top to bottom. Like a mountain splitting in two, one half of the tower lurched away from the other half, and the temple on top of the tower, Dur Anki, shattered with an earsplitting explosion and fell into the chasm along with the golden sun disk.

A vast and dense cloud of dust now obliterated the ruined tower from view as tens of thousands of people, grouped according to tribes and ethnicities, streamed out of the city in every direction, never to return.

Gasping, Reza and Vashti turned and gazed at each other, then turned to join their families.

In the sky above Babylon Chulgomet and the remaining spirit lords grimly assessed the situation.

"We are undone again! We are monkeys on leashes!" screeched Asmodeus.

"Not so!" answered Chulgomet. "The fact that the Creator felt it necessary to cause the abandoning of Babylon indicates our success at leading the humans away from him. He is threatened by us, but he will not destroy us!

"Look Colleagues," he continued, "the vortex is emptied! The spirits have mingled with their assigned people groups. The people will wander wherever they will go. They will settle down and build cities and populate the Earth. And as long as they are endowed with free wills we will have many to worship us."

Chulgomet gazed down on the desperate and misguided masses of humanity below him, scurrying like frantic insects.

"The principle remains," he concluded.

"AS ABOVE, SO BELOW!"

The exodus from Babylon appeared to be a chaotic affair, humanly speaking. The tribes and ethnicities of mankind streamed out of the city in every direction as if driven by the lash of an invisible taskmaster. They could not even recall what it was that had held them there in the first place. The only thought now was to find a new home somewhere. Tens of thousands of souls wandered away from everything they had ever known, not knowing where they went.

Chulgomet and the other fallen spirit lords watched grimly from another dimension. They had succeeded in leading the masses of humanity away from the Creator again, and had thoroughly corrupted the majority of men and women. It was also true that the vortex over Babylon had emptied itself and myriads of spirits had gone to infiltrate the tribes of the earth and go with them wherever they went. Their goals were to steal from them what was good in their lives, kill them, and destroy God's human and earthly creation. Steal, kill, and destroy. But there was a price to pay. The spirits themselves were further corrupted, both in their appearance and powers. No longer could they appear physically or communicate directly with humans. However, they could still make psychic impressions on them, and could, in that way, instill misdirected thoughts and teachings.

More than ever, the fallen spirits were enthused by the shedding of human blood. Thus, a key element in their strategies was to incite violence and warfare. Over every battlefield in the ages to come, the fallen spirits would flock like vultures, gleefully encouraging the carnage. Of special delight to them was violence committed in the name of religion; for they would be the driving force behind every inquisition and persecution throughout history, behind every sword-induced conversion, behind every killing in the name of God.

As the tribes wandered and eventually settled down, they would be known for centuries to come by the name of their ancestral patriarchs. Noah had three sons: Shem, Ham, and Japheth. Their ancestors now made up the tribes of mankind. Broadly speaking, the ancestors of Shem, through his sons Elam, Ashur, Arphaxad, Lud, and Aram, settled in what would be known generally as the Middle East. The ancestors of Ham, through his sons Cush, Mizraim, Put, and Canaan, migrated into Israel, Lebanon, and Africa. Finally, the ancestors of Japheth, through his sons Gomer, Magog, Madai, Javan, Tubal, Meshech, and Tiras, migrated northwest into Europe and north and east into the furthest reaches of Asia.

What would continue unabated over the centuries to come would be the rebellion of fallen spirits and humans toward the only Creator God. Since humans and spirits were endowed with free wills, they would be held accountable for their rebellion and sins. Their thoughts, words, intentions, and actions would determine the state of their existence in the ages to come. The fallen spirits spread their teaching over all the earth that one could achieve salvation through certain good works; by building ones' own stairway to heaven. God knew that humans could not save themselves; they needed a Savior. God himself would provide one, in the strangest way conceivable.

At the predetermined time, a child named Yahshua, or Jesus, was born to a virgin in Israel. The child was born in a town called Bethlehem, which meant 'The House of Bread'. When the child was grown he said to the people "I am the Bread of life, come down from heaven." By his life, death, and resurrection he condemned sin and death and made a way of atonement for humanity, so that whoever came to him in faith would be forgiven of their sins and reconciled with a perfect God.

The love nature of God was physically manifested on the earth.

His love came down.

As above, so below.

To order additional books,
or for information regarding speaking
engagements
go to:
www.mysterybabylon.org

or contact:
Frontera Publishing Company at
info@mysterybabylon.org

or by mail at:
Frontera Publishing Company
P.O. Box 80112
Austin, Texas 78708